RED DOVE

By Kathy Long

For my mother, and all the hours she spent helping me learn to write...

Chapter 1

Rachel sighed and ran her fingers through her long red hair as she blew a deep breath out. She looked around and the mess on the floor and called out to her friend in the next room. "Sara, how are you doing in there?"

Sara raced around the corner swatting a spider web from her face. "It is so gross in here. Bugs are everywhere! I'm covered in spider webs! Every time I try to measure something a spider scares me to death, and I drop the measuring tape!"

"Well, it's an old house. What do you expect?" Rachel said.

"You'd think the last people who owned this house never heard of Raid," Sara snapped back. "Are you sure this is the right place?"

"Yes, Sara. It's perfect. Well, it will be once we knock out that wall over there and paint it," Rachel said, pointing toward the dividing wall between a living room and den. The house, built in the 1930s, was nestled in downtown Memphis, and Rachel had talked Sara into buying it to expand their consulting business into a full-fledged advertising agency. Sara's personal credit had taken quite a hit over the years, so Rachel wound up putting the house in her name only. The two had been working all day to take measurements and draw up a floor plan that worked to house their new employees in an inviting and creative environment.

"Did you talk to Sam Hardin today about his website?" Sara asked.

"Yeah, he is still working on getting concept approval for the final architecture of the site. We've got the photo shoot with him and Richard in the morning," Rachel answered as she piled the pencil, ruler and paper in the floor by the door to the main room.

"I hope he gets that architecture approved. I've got copy written for the sections we discussed already. I can modify them, but it's a lot of work," Sara said.

"I know. It will work out. We still have 8 more weeks to finish before the launch."

"And I need two of those for testing," Sara argued as she threw her supplies down next to Rachel's.

"I know, I know. I'll get it for you," Rachel said, patting Sara on the back to ease her fears.

"What time is the crew coming tomorrow?" Sara asked, referring to the construction crew set to knock out the wall and begin repairs.

"Johnny said not until after 10. It will probably be a long day again tomorrow, so you want to call it a night?"

"What? At 7:30? Really? Rachel Parks is ready to quit? What is the world coming to?" Sara teased. In addition to being the visionary and a creative spirit, her friend and business partner Rachel was a workaholic.

"Oh, stop it. You know you are dying to do this expansion as much as I am," Rachel said, brushing the dust off her black jeans.

"It is kind of exciting. It's our dream finally coming true," Sara said and then paused. "We are going to be able to do this, right?"

"Piece of cake," Rachel said, putting her arm around Sara and leading her over to the door where their purses were hanging.

"My friend Rachel, the eternal optimist," Sara said rolling her eyes.

"No, piece of cake. I want one. Let's go to The Arcade for dinner," Rachel smiled.

"You buy the cake. You owe me for sending me into the room with all the spider webs!"

The two laughed and grabbed their purses as they exited the house. Rachel flipped the lights off and locked the door. She smiled as she thought about all the years she had put in at the bottom of the pile at agencies and the years she and Rachel had spent trying to build a business. This was finally happening. A full-service agency. Their full-service agency.

Chapter 2

As Sara and Rachel entered the restaurant, they found it hopping with business as usual for a Thursday night in downtown Memphis. A waitress with a nose ring and rose tattoos on her left arm passed by the door on the way to serve three trays of food and slowed long enough to say, "Sit wherever you like, girls."

Rachel scoped the restaurant and saw an open booth in the corner facing the train station. She walked quickly to it, pulling Sara's arm all the way. The two plopped down in the booth, the springs nearly gone, and the colors faded on the vinyl upholstery. The table was covered in speckled linoleum and edged in stainless – Rachel assumed it was a look popular in the late 50s. The table had an array of condiments and a napkin holder. A young man raced by, sliding waters on the table for Rachel and Sara on his way to the kitchen. Rachel grabbed the menu stuck under the napkin holder and started to peruse it. "What are you going to have?" she asked Sara.

"My usual," Sara answered.

"Shocking," Rachel said under her breath. Sara was painfully predictable and was always eating healthy. It annoyed Rachel that Sara was so buttoned up with her eating. She liked to taste new things and try different dishes. She scoped the menu for something she had never tried, hoping it would gross Sara out.

"You girls know what you want?" An older woman said as she walked toward the table, smacking her gum. She balanced a dirty plate on one hip while she grabbed her pencil out of her apron along with a notepad. Her jeans had more holes than Rachel thought was fashionable, and the bun was coming out of her hair.

Sara nodded, "Grilled chicken salad, hold the tomato, with balsamic vinaigrette on the side, please."

The woman wrote furiously, and then looked at Rachel and nodded, "And for you, honey?"

"Mmmmm, the Monte Cristo, please, with chili cheese fries and French onion soup," Rachel answered as she slid the menu under the napkin holder. Rachel was pleased to see Sara's nose wrinkle out of the corner of her eye.

"Ok, girls. I'll be right back. I'm Janice if you need something," the waitress said as she turned on her platform heels and walked to the kitchen. Rachel wondered how anyone walked in those, much less worked at a restaurant. She had made the mistake of purchasing the cutest pair of black platform boots last fall. One trip to the office cured her of wanting to wear them anywhere she had to walk. She had nearly stumbled into the pavement at Front and Union and garnered blisters that lasted for two weeks.

"I'm thinking we can make the front parlor into our conference room. It's big enough and offers the most in terms of décor for our customers," Rachel offered.

"We'll have to get a bigger table," Sara said.

A handsome police officer emerged from the bar area and walked toward Sara and Rachel. He sat down next to Rachel, "You don't need a bigger table. I can't stay long anyway, ladies; I'm on duty."

Rachel's face flooded with a smile. Todd and Rachel met months ago at her church when she was working a local art fundraiser to benefit foster children. There was instant chemistry between the two of them, and Todd had been chasing Rachel ever since that night. His patrol was in the neighborhood, and he took his time whenever he passed their current business, hoping to catch a glimpse and talk to Rachel. "So now you are spying on us? Are we under investigation?" Rachel teased.

Todd let his boyish grin shine as he stared right at Rachel. "As a matter of fact, you are," he said, locking his gaze to her green eyes. "I've had my eye on you for a while now."

"I may have to take this up with your supervisor," Rachel flirted back.

Sara rolled her eyes.

"You want to call him? Here is his number," Todd joked back, pulling out his pen and writing his own phone number on a napkin. "I think he can meet with you tomorrow for dinner. 7pm?"

"I don't date cops," Rachel protested.

Todd stood up, put his hands on the table and leaned down to look into Rachel's eyes again. He had waited a long time to ask her out, and he wasn't going to take no for an answer. He paused and then confidently said, "Dinner. 7pm. Text me the address, and I'll pick you up."

Rachel felt goose bumps run over her arms. She started to protest again, but Sara kicked her under the table. She squinted her eyes at Sara in disapproval. Todd smiled, knowing he was making an impression. He walked quickly to the door and turned back once last time and pointed to Rachel. "7pm!" he shouted as he left the building, hoping the chemistry he felt would be enough to make her say yes.

"What are you doing?" Rachel asked Sara in a huff.

"What? He's cute," Sara said.

"He is cute," Rachel smiled again, totally smitten with him. The smile disappeared suddenly. "But I don't date cops!" Rachel said, squishing the napkin into a ball.

Sara rescued the napkin from her and shoved it into her own purse. "You don't date cops. You don't date doctors. You don't date lawyers. I've known you for nearly a decade, and I haven't seen you go out on more than a handful of dates," Sara chided.

"That's because dates lead to other things. My momma always said, 'be careful who you date, as you might end up marrying them.'" Rachel said. "And I don't want to be married to a cop."

"He didn't ask you to marry him - just have dinner with him. It took him like 4 months to finally ask you, so don't blow it. Have some fun," Sara ordered. "It won't kill you to let a man pay for your meal every once in a while."

Rachel sighed. She put her elbow on the table and rested her head in the palm of her hand thinking of his deep brown eyes and muscular build. She did like Todd. She knew he stopped by more than he should at their office. And he had been out to more than a few of her church outreach events. She more than enjoyed flirting with him. Rachel smiled and said, "Maybe just one date."

Chapter 3

Rachel slammed her keys on the foyer table of her downtown loft apartment and dumped her purse and briefcase next to them. She went to the bedroom and kicked off her shoes near the bed. She grabbed the television remote and started to click it on when she remembered she forgot to send an email to Richard with the approved list of props for tomorrow's photo shoot. She walked back to the foyer to retrieve her phone and realized it was missing. She didn't use it at the restaurant. She must have left it at the new office. Rachel squished her nose and tried to decide if it was worth it to go back tonight or if it could wait until the morning. She didn't like leaving things undone. And she didn't like early mornings. Going by the office on the way to the shoot meant leaving early. It would be better to go back tonight and get it over with, she thought. Rachel grabbed her shoes from the bedroom and headed out only with her keys and wallet in hand.

Downtown Memphis wasn't the safest place after dark, but she lived and worked in the area, so she was familiar with what to watch for and how to avoid the riff raff. She pulled her blue 1969 Mustang with white racing stripes into the driveway of her new business home and turned off the engine. She enjoyed driving a car that grabbed attention, but she had forgotten how loud the engine was at night. She didn't want to start out on the wrong foot with her neighbors, as this area was still mostly residential even though the zoning had recently changed new property transfers to mixed use. She had found the house for sale in a cheap estate liquidation and thought it would be perfect for her needs, and her budget.

Rachel climbed out of the car and headed for the door. She caught a glimpse of movement in the front parlor window and stopped, wondering if there was danger lurking inside. A yell came from behind her, and she turned to see three teenagers throwing a basketball as they walked down the street. It must have been their shadows, she thought. She continued to the door, unlocking it and flipping on a light as she entered. Instantly, she saw her phone lying on the floor in the middle of the den area and moved to get it. "There you are," she said out loud, as if the phone could hear her. As she bent over to retrieve the phone, a man emerged from the parlor room and ran to the door, slamming it as he exited. Rachel heard the noise and chased the intruder out the door. She flung it open and caught his shadow disappear around the corner. "Hey!" she yelled out, but it was no use. He was gone, and she didn't even get a good look at him.

Rachel's first instinct was to call the police. She clicked her phone on and started pressing the buttons. After she hit the "9" key, she stopped suddenly. Was this really a life-threatening emergency? The intruder ran away and is long gone. There wasn't anything to steal in the house, not yet at least. They hadn't even finished the construction, much less put anything of value in the house. She flipped the lights on in the rest of the house. She walked around, checking for clues or damage. If nothing was broken or taken, what exactly were the police going to do for her anyway, she wondered. Memphis was a crime-ridden city, and the police had plenty of other real crimes to take care of than chase a mystery squatter or teen prankster. Plus, Todd worked this side of town. Rachel thought about that for a minute. The thought of seeing him in action was interesting, but then again, she didn't want to look helpless or ridiculous to him. After finding nothing of interest in the house to suggest a real crime other than illegal entry, Rachel turned the lights off and locked the door behind her. She got into her car and started home.

The drive back to her apartment was quiet, as she pondered her intruder's intentions and wondered if she had done the right thing by not alerting the police. She decided they needed an alarm system before putting anything of value in the house, but crime was part of being downtown. That's what insurance was for, she thought.

Rachel pulled into the parking garage and parked in her spot on the third floor. She exited the vehicle and walked toward the elevator. She punched the button to go down and opened the email app on her phone. She typed out a message to Richard giving final approval on prop list number two for the photo shoot and hit send as the doors opened. She stepped inside and rode the elevator down to the ground floor. Rachel walked across the street and entered her building using the key pad entry. She rounded the corner and headed for her apartment.

Chapter 4

Rodney entered the room slowly, careful to notice the two Italian bodyguards on either side of the entrance. "You have news for me?" asked a gruff voice belonging to a heavy-set man in his fifties barked from behind a desk without looking up from his work. The lights had been dimmed, but Rodney could still tell that his boss had been working late in his home office. He hadn't broken out the cigar yet, a sure sign that business had wrapped up for the evening.

Rodney chose his words carefully. "Nothing, Boss. He went to the old lady's house, but was interrupted."

"Interrupted?" he asked, again continuing his work.

"Yeah, some woman came in. She must have bought the house."

"Did he find it?" the man asked as he looked up from his papers.

"No. And my guys went back after she left. It's not there, Boss."

The man stood and threw his pen down on the desk. "He's been out two days! Two days!" he shouted while rubbing his head in frustration. "If he went there, he knows something."

"Can't we just pick him up? This would be a lot easier if we just beat it out of him," Rodney offered.

"Like you did the old lady?" the man shouted. "If anyone is torturing someone, it's going to be me. You got it?"

A young woman dressed in a maid's uniform appeared in the doorway with a tray and a dinner plate. "I'm sorry, sir. I thought you were ready for your dinner," she said as she turned to leave.

"Yes, yes, bring it in. If Mr. Brown here doesn't ruin my appetite, it will be a miracle," the man said sarcastically.

The woman brought in the tray and sat it on the coffee table in front of the leather sofa. She gave a smirk to Rodney as she passed him. The two men silently watched her arrange the items on the table and leave before continuing their conversation.

Rodney was silent a little while longer while the man came out from behind the desk and approached him. He put his arm around Rodney and whispered in his ear. "He went there first. He knows something."

"Maybe." Rodney regretted it as soon as he uttered the word.

"Maybe?" the man asked as he squinted his eyes.

"M – M- Maybe J.P. doesn't know where it is either?" Rodney said, trying to cover his tracks.

"Then find the girl. Find the red dove and bring me the box. Or I'll gut you like this fish," the man said as he sat down to eat his dinner. As Rodney started to leave, the man raised his fork up and yelled out, "And do it quietly. No mess. No cops!"

Chapter 5

Rachel pulled into the drive at the new business just after 3pm. The sun was brutally hot, and the humidity had to be nearly 100%. Rachel loathed Memphis summers. She had put an aftermarket air conditioning unit in her Mustang, but it was no match for Memphis in July. Rachel put the car in park and climbed out, her legs sticking to the leather seats. She could feel the sweat on her neck already and let out a silent "ick." Pulling her hair back into a ponytail, she grabbed her things and entered the house.

Sara met her at the door. "Did you see the look on Richard's face when Sam knocked that light over? I thought he was going to pop a blood vessel and bleed all over us!"

Rachel chuckled, "Yeah. Fortunately, it landed on the carpet, so it wasn't a big deal. Richard is just a nervous nelly."

"I would be, too, if that were my equipment, and the client was that clumsy."

"I think he was more put out with Sam's need to direct everything. Like he didn't trust us – or Richard."

"Oh, totally!" Sara rolled her eyes as she reached in her pocket and pulled out the napkin from The Arcade. "Here. Text him your address."

"What? No, I'm not going to text him!" Rachel screamed.

Sara grabbed Rachel by the arm and lowered her voice. "Yes, you are. You said last night – "

"I said I didn't date cops," Rachel interrupted.

"And then you said maybe one date," Sara reminded her. Sara held out the napkin with Todd's digits showing.

"No, I'm not going to text him!"

"Come on! He's cute, Rachel. He likes you. What else do you need to have dinner?"

"I need him to reflect Jesus."

Sara sighed. "For a date? How about him reflecting being a gentleman?"

"He's a cop, and a flirt. I doubt he knows how to be a gentleman."

"He doesn't flirt with me. Besides, I think you enjoy sparring with him."

"A little," Rachel admitted with the faintest hint of a smile. She pushed past Sara and sat her things down on the floor. "Did you get lunch? I'm starving," she said as she made her way to the kitchen.

19

"Yeah – from Mr. Won's."

Rachel made a plate of Kung Pow chicken and white rice. She dug in the plastic grocery sacks to find that Sara had gotten Diet Coke. Rachel hated Diet Coke, or anything diet. But it would have to do. She hopped upon the counter and started to eat. When she was nearly finished, Sara came back in holding Rachel's phone. "Todd says to wear green because it brings out your eyes."

Rachel spit out her diet coke and nearly dropped her plate on the floor. "What? You didn't! Tell me you didn't text him my address!"

Sara turned and ran down the hall.

Rachel hopped off the counter and started chasing her. "Sara! Sara! Did you tell him I'd go out with him tonight? You better be kidding!"

"Of course, I'm kidding." Sara said as she stopped running to face Rachel.

Rachel suddenly looked disappointed. "Well, good," she said unconvincingly and turned to walk back to her lunch.

Sara noticed her change in countenance and tried to capitalize on it. "I have the most beautiful green dress you can borrow." Rachel kept walking. "It would be perfect on you. It's too long for me, but you have such long legs." Rachel entered the kitchen and picked up her food. "He really likes you, Rachel. Just one date."

Rachel ignored her and resumed eating her food. "You can send me a cryptic text if you aren't having a good time, and I'll call and save you. I promise."

Rachel looked up. "Do you promise?"

Sara nodded and handed her the phone and the napkin. Rachel took both, paused, and then handed them back. "I can't do it. You do it."

Sara was giddy as a school girl. "Yay!" she shouted with glee as she jumped up and down. Rachel laughed at her friend's silliness and felt a little sick at her stomach.

Sara punched in the numbers and started to text Rachel's address to Todd. "Wait!" Rachel said. "Text him from your phone."

"What? Why?"

"Because if the date is bad, then you can get all the follow-up phone calls!"

Sara rolled her eyes. "Fine." Sara texted Todd from her phone: 101 Tennessee Street. Suite 105. 7pm.

"Now can we get to work?" Rachel asked as if she was annoyed.

"Yeah, I think we need to start with the colors in the conference room. I have the paint chips in there from our initial ideas."

Rachel sat her food down and followed Sara into what was going to be the conference room. The two of them held up different paint chips, trying to decide what looked best with the natural light. As they narrowed their choices, Johnny entered the room.

"Um, Ms. Rachel," he started.

"Yeah, Johnny," she answered without turning her attention away front the paint chips.

"Um, we are finished knocking out the wall. My guys have put up the beam for support we talked about, but there isn't much more we can do today," he said. Johnny had done several jobs for Rachel over the course of her career in terms of sets and construction. He always insisted upon putting a "Ms." in front of her name, but she didn't much care for it. It made her feel old and awkward.

"Ok, thanks, Johnny. See you tomorrow. Thanks for your work today," Rachel said.

"Yes, ma'am," he said, ducking out of the room. His crew was already packing up their tools for the day.

Sara and Rachel kept looking at colors until all the crew was gone. Suddenly, Rachel stopped looking at the walls and turned to Sara. "Oh, I can't do this today."

"You can't do what?" Sara asked.

"This! Paint!" She said, exacerbated, throwing the paint chips in the air.

"Why not? You don't like the colors?" Sara asked. Rachel wasn't usually melodramatic.

"No, it's not that." Rachel paused. "All I can think about is this stupid date you got me into tonight."

"Yeah?" Sara asked, so excited she could barely contain herself.

"Yeah! I'm so mad at you right now!"

"Come on. Let's go. We'll go get your nails done, and I'll grab that dress from my house on the way to your apartment and help you get ready." Sara said.

"My nails? Really? The last time I had my nails done was for your wedding." Rachel protested. Rachel was a tom boy. She had a tall, curvy physique and long wavy red hair that she wore mostly down. She dressed up for client meetings, but she wasn't much on being a girlie girl. Her makeup was minimalist at best. The thought of getting dolled up to go out with a cop did not amuse her.

"Exactly. Come on; it'll be fun. A girls' day. For me."

Rachel started to say no and realized how excited Sara was. "Fine. It's not like I'm going to get any work done today anyway," Rachel said, frustrated.

Rachel bent down to grab her things and noticed a wooden box on top of her stuff. "Is this your box?" Rachel picked it up to inspect it, noticing that it had a very intricate carving of an angel on it.

"No, Johnny found it in the wall, and I told him to leave it with your stuff. You like that kind of thing more than I do."

"In the wall? That's weird." Rachel said.

"Yeah, it's kind of cool. This house is old. Probably some kid put it there when they built the house."

"It is pretty nice. Maybe Todd can tell me about the design. He carves, you know?" Rachel said as she turned the box upside down, checking out the construction of it.

"Carves? Oh yeah, you met him at that art thing at church. An artist cop. hmmmm." Sara pondered. "A hot artist cop," she said with a huge grin.

"Stop it, already." Rachel snapped.

"And now you have something to talk about on your first date," Sara said with a smile.

Rachel ignored her and opened the box. "It's empty."

"Yeah, I was hoping for some long-lost love letter or something, but it's just a toy I guess."

"I guess. Ok, let's go." Rachel put the box down in her purse and gathered her other things.

Chapter 6

Rachel and Sara arrived back at her apartment about 5. "We have to hurry!" Sara said.

"What? We've got like two hours. How long does it take you to get ready anyway?" Sara ignored Rachel and pulled a flat iron out of her bag along with a brush, curlers, hair clips, hair spray, mousse, and a massive makeup kit. "Sara, I'm not going to use all that stuff, you know?"

"I know. As soon as we decide on straight or curly, I'll put half of it back." Sara answered, oblivious to Rachel's aversion to typical female beauty treatments.

Rachel rolled her eyes. "Fine. Straight."

Sara looked at Rachel and squinted her eyes. "Yeah, I think that's a good call. It will look nice with your hair draping on your bare shoulders."

"What? The dress is strapless? Sara, I – " Rachel protested.

Sara interrupted her. "Calm down, Rachel. It's off the shoulder."

Rachel rolled her eyes again and sarcastically said, "Oh yeah, much better."

Sara proceeded to plug in her flat iron and lay out the makeup kit. She chose a green eye shadow and heavy mascara. "I think we need to go classic red on the lips."

Rachel rarely wore that much makeup. "Do you want me to look like a hooker?"

"Come on, Rachel. I know what I'm doing." Sara whined.

"Ok, you win. Do your worst," Rachel caved. Sara spent the next hour and a half working on Rachel's hair and makeup to get it just the way she wanted it. She offered Rachel the dress and shoes and told her to go change. Rachel emerged from the bathroom, and Sara clapped.

"You look radiant!" she said, pleased with her look. Sara looked at her watch and quickly packed up her stuff. "I'm going to be late. I've got to pick up Josh from swim team."

"You are going to leave me here?" Rachel asked.

"You look so fabulous! My work here is done!" Sara said as she blew Rachel a kiss and left the apartment.

Rachel turned toward the mirror and studied herself. She gave a half smile, but she was uncomfortable. She thought the look was nice, but not her usual self. She looked more like she was going to a wedding than on a date. She wondered what Todd would think of this version of herself. She took the 4" heels off and wandered into her closet. She picked through the clothes until she found something that fit her style better. She grabbed her favorite pair of twill black pants and a blue V-neck tunic with embellishments that hugged her curves, but not too tightly. She pulled out black lace-up oxfords with a 2" heel and a denim jacket. She laid the new outfit on the bed and checked the clock. She had time for a shower. She felt badly that Sara had gone to so much trouble, but she needed to feel like herself or this wasn't going to work. She hopped in the shower and washed the hair product out of her hair and the makeup off her face. She quickly dried off and dressed in her own clothes. She dried and brushed her hair and used minimal makeup from her own small collection. She took a check in the full-length mirror. Pleased with her choice, she quickly hung the green dress in her closet.

Rachel picked up a couple of empty glasses that she and Sara had used while working on her hair and made sure the apartment was straightened. She was planning to do her weekly clean on Saturday as always, but she liked to keep things in order. The knock on the door came at 6:58. Rachel made a loop around the couch on her way to answer the door. She didn't want to appear too anxious. As she opened the door, she wondered if she had made the right choice with her look. Todd stood at the door holding a small handful of flowers and showing off a huge boyish smile. He held the flowers out toward Rachel who accepted them with a smile.

The flowers were unusual, Rachel thought. Not your typical rose formation or spring collection found at the supermarket. "Thank you. Let me just put these in water," she said as she motioned for him to come in while she put them in water. "You didn't have to do that, you know?"

"Well, I wanted to see the inside of your apartment and figured you would invite me in if I brought you flowers," Todd said with a smile.

Rachel chuckled and said, "Ah, an honest man." After putting the flowers in a vase of water, she turned and grabbed her purse off the counter as well as the box with the angel carving Johnny's crew had found in the new office and waved Todd toward the door. "Shall we?"

"Absolutely!" Todd said as held the door for her and let it close behind them.

She reached across him to lock the deadbolt and said, "All set now."

Todd walked beside her. "My car is on the curb up here. The black Challenger."

Rachel smiled. He had been to church outreach events off duty, but she never paid attention to his car. "Nice," she said. "Hemi?"

"You bet."

Rachel laughed. "It's not what's under the hood but who's behind the wheel," she joked.

"No argument there," Todd said as he opened the door for Rachel and helped her in. He walked around the backside of the car, climbed in and started the engine. He could see Rachel liked the roar of the engine. Todd peeled out of the space and made a 180-degree turn, careful not to bark the tires too much. He didn't want to appear as a show-off.

As they pulled into the parking lot at Arthur's, Rachel pulled out the box and started to explain to Todd why she brought it. "My construction manager found this in the wall of the house at the new office. I thought you might like it."

Todd glanced over at it and took it with his right hand. "I do. It's got a beautiful Picasso-esque quality to it."

"Yeah, the angel is a little deformed I think," Rachel said.

"This was in the wall at your new office?" Todd asked.

"Yeah. I have no idea why." Rachel took the box back from Todd and put it in his back seat. "We can look at it later. Let's not miss the sunset."

Dinner at Arthur's came with a beautiful patio view of the city and the Memphis bridge just as the sun set over the river. The one-line sparing continued intermittently throughout dinner, but most of the conversation was genuine. Todd found Rachel fascinating and her passion for art and others unmeasurable. "Tell me what the best part of the church art ministry is," Todd said.

"It has to be when they get to make their own creations. After we've done all the techniques, I let them pick their favorite and make a project of their own choosing. It's amazing what these kids can do, even the ones that aren't gifted as artists. They are all so creative and imaginative. There is something about being a kid that just is freeing in terms of thought. I guess they aren't concerned about what others think yet or consumed with the worries of this world," Rachel said. Her eyes lit up when she talked about her work or her ministry at church, and Todd loved seeing her so animated.

"Part of why Jesus said you had to be like little children to come to Him, I suppose," Todd answered.

Rachel thought about that for a second. "Makes sense. We get so wrapped up in the worry of this world at times that we lose focus on what's truly important."

As they continued, Todd shared tidbits about his work as she requested, careful not to dive too deeply into the danger he faced every day on the job. There was more to Todd than the job, and he was interested in a slow, long woo of Rachel, not one in which he shined as a hero at first but the flame burned out quickly after the realization that he wasn't all that.

After dinner, Todd asked. "Are you up for some loud, redneck fun?"

Rachel smiled. "What did you have in mind?"

"Open quarter mile races at the motorsports park."

30

"Only if you race."

Todd thought about that for a minute. "You riding shotgun?"

"Wouldn't miss it."

Now this was a great first date, they both thought.

Chapter 7

At the races, Todd raced as he promised with Rachel riding shotgun. They lost miserably to another Mopar, a Barracuda with a hopped-up engine. It didn't surprise either of them, as the pairing was random, not based on class size or horsepower. "Well, maybe it is a little about what is under the hood," Rachel said through laughter after they cleared the race lane, turned in their borrowed helmets and headed to the parking lot.

"That was pretty pathetic, huh?" Todd laughed.

Rachel stopped laughing and said with a straight face, "Oh, no, I loved every second of it. Promise me we'll do it again sometime?"

Todd offered his hand out, and Rachel took it. "You are an interesting lady, Rachel Parks." Rachel was embarrassed but pleased. They rode in silence back to her apartment. Rachel was smiling the whole way. She was smitten with Todd for sure. She looked over at him from time to time, wondering what this man saw in her. Todd pulled up to the curb and put the car in park. "Want to see something I've been working on?"

"Sure," Rachel agreed.

"Ok, but if I miss you have to promise not to laugh. Deal?"

"Deal," Rachel agreed, wondering what he was planning.

Todd exited the car, took three steps back, got a running go and slid across the hood of the car on his left hip. He landed slightly off balance on the same leg and stepped up on the curb to control himself. He held his arms up in the air, looking for a reaction from Rachel.

Rachel realized her mouth was wide open. She clapped and said, "I'm going to have to deduct half a point for that dismount, but pretty solid technique."

Todd laughed and opened her door to let her out. He grabbed her hand and led her into the apartment building. As they rounded the corner, Rachel dropped Todd's hand and started to fish for her keys. Suddenly, she turned back, "Oh, I left that box in your car."

Todd smiled, "I'll give it to you on our next date."

"Next date? Who said there was going to be a next date?"

"You did, when you didn't have your friend Sara interrupt this one," Todd said with a confident smile.

Somewhat amused that he could figure that out, Rachel laughed and said, "Goodnight, Todd," as she opened the door and entered her apartment.

"Goodnight, Rachel."

Rachel closed the door and smiled as she fell into it, sliding to the floor. Todd was a nice guy. He was witty and charming, and it didn't hurt that he was easy on the eyes. She let her mind linger on the conversation and his charm for a few seconds. And then she remembered, he's a cop. And Rachel didn't want to marry a cop. Another date with Todd would be dangerous; she liked him more than she thought she might. Rachel put her things down and started to get ready for bed, hoping she could sleep, her mind racing of with all the what ifs about Todd. Cop or not, she wanted to pursue this more.

Chapter 8

The sound of footsteps from the apartment above her woke Rachel up on Saturday morning around 8. Living on the bottom floor had its advantages, and this was definitely not one of them. She tried to shut out the noise and go back to sleep, but it was useless. She was awake and her mind buzzing with thoughts of what she needed to do today. And of Todd. Rachel rolled out of the bed and headed for the shower. She stepped into the shower with a huge smile on her face. She enjoyed herself with Todd, and she allowed the magic of last evening to fill her mind.

After finishing her shower, Rachel put on a pair of jeans and a turquoise blouse. She entered the kitchen area and began digging in the refrigerator for some sort of leftovers to munch on. She liked breakfast, but wasn't much on getting up early enough to cook it most mornings, so she had a habit of eating leftovers as her opening meal for the day. Rachel grabbed some Chinese food from a couple of nights ago, warmed it in the microwave and sat down to enjoy it along with a glass of tea. She grabbed her phone and punched up her emails. Pleasantly surprised that she didn't have client emails, Rachel engrossed herself reading her daily devotion as she finished her breakfast. Rachel laughed when she realized the passage was from Matthew 18, the same passage which Todd had referred to last night in terms of becoming like children. She was amused at God's humor. Rachel spent just a couple of minutes in prayer, asking God for wisdom regarding Todd. She admitted to God silently that she was attracted to him, but asked Him to help her guard her heart. After finishing up, she cleared the table, put on her black sandals and headed for the door. She grabbed her purse and keys and locked the door behind her.

As she headed to the garage, the phone rang. Sara. She'd want to know all the details from last night. Rachel slid the phone to "ignore" the call and kept walking. Her phone buzzed with a voicemail and then a text: Call me about last night. Rachel grumbled, knowing she'd eventually have to share something with Sara.

Rachel threw her phone in the passenger seat along with her purse and headed to her new office. She wondered if Johnny's crew was already working on patching the ceiling. As she rounded the corner near the new office house, Rachel saw Sara's car behind Johnny's work van. Rachel knew she'd have to come clean with Sara about what happened last night if she wanted to get anything done today. Sara would be relentless. Rachel pulled into the driveway and parked next to Sara. She grabbed her things and entered the house.

"It's about time, sleepy head. I've been dying to hear all about your date last night with the hot cop!" Sara greeted her from across the room.

Ignoring the comment, Rachel walked toward the den area and started talking with Johnny, "How is it coming?" she asked.

"We will be done today with the patchwork. We should be able to paint by Monday, so we need your colors today to order the paint," Johnny answered.

"Got it," Rachel said as she inspected their progress. Rachel walked up to the removed wall area and stared at the support beam put in its place. She was happy with where the renovations were going.

Just then, Sara leaned around Rachel and put her face in front of Rachel's. "We need to talk!"

Rachel turned and walked toward the parlor room, "No, we don't. You just want juicy gossip!"

"Exactly," Sara said. "Come on, Rachel, you know I live vicariously through you when it comes to this stuff. You gotta give me a fix!" Sara pleaded. Sara had married her high school sweetheart Jason right after college. She had a decent marriage, but they were past the honeymoon stage and focused more on the chores of the partnership than romance most of the time. Rachel thought it was a shame, as Sara had a lot of creative energy that she could use to spice things up if she would put the effort into her own relationship and leave Rachel's love life alone.

"What? It was fine. It was a date. That's all," Rachel said.

"It was fine? It was 'fine'? Really? So, that glow I see around you doesn't have anything to do with last night?" Sara questioned.

"I don't glow. And no, it does not," Rachel protested.

Sara could detect her friend's inner happiness. "Me thinks thou doeth protest too much," Sara said.

Rachel grinned. She wanted to hold it in, but she couldn't. "Ok, it was fantastic!"

"Yeah?" Sara squealed with a huge smile on her face. "Where did he take you? The Peabody? The Four Seasons?"

Sara liked the finer things in life. Rachel was more down-to-earth. "He's a cop; not a Wall Street executive, Sara. We went to Arthur's and then to the races in West Memphis."

"The races? –" Sara was horrified at first, and then thought how much Rachel probably liked that. "And?"

"And – and, it was fun. He's a nice guy." Rachel said with a smile that told Sara there was much more to it than that.

"You are killing me!" Sara said, exacerbated. "Come on, Rachel, give me something."

"Ok, fine. He's awesome. We had a great time. I really like him –" Rachel stopped talking suddenly, dropped her smile and said, "which is why I can't see him again."

"What? You like him, but you aren't going to see him again?" Sara yelled.

"No," Rachel said as she turned away from Sara. She was a terrible liar, and Sara would be able to read her expression. "You know I don't date cops."

"Rachel?" Sara paused for the answer that didn't come. She grabbed Rachel by the arm and spun her back around. "You are going out with him again, aren't you?"

Rachel smiled and said nothing.

"Yes!" Sara shouted with glee. "Is he a good kisser?" she asked like a school girl.

"I don't know. I didn't kiss him," Rachel said proudly.

"You are incorrigible!" Sara yelled. "You wouldn't tell me if you did, would you?"

"Nope!" Rachel said with a smirk. "Enough about all that. We need to nail these colors down."

"Fine!" Sara grunted. The two of them retreated to the new conference room area and began deciding on colors. Every few minutes, Sara had to try hard not to bite her tongue. She didn't get the details from Rachel that she craved, but she knew better than to push her friend too hard. She focused on the task at hand, hoping that a lunch break might help Rachel ease up on the sharing details.

Suddenly, Sara's phone buzzed with a text. "It's from him! You didn't give him your real number?"

Rachel could hardly contain her excitement. "What does it say?"

"Sunday, 5:45 at the corner of Front and Tennessee if you ever want to see the box again." Sara read, confused.

Rachel laughed out loud, much to her friend's dismay, and thought for a minute what to reply. The corner of Front and Tennessee was where her apartment building was located.

"What does that mean?" Sara asked.

"Oh, it's just a joke. Text him back, 'I want proof of life first'," Rachel said, pleased with the game.

Sara thought it was odd, but did as she was asked. "What box?"

"You know, the box Johnny found. Remember? You suggested I share it with him. I left it in his car, and he's holding it hostage until I go out with him again." Rachel said, smiling from ear to ear.

"Y'all are weird!" Sara said.

Rachel took Sara's phone out of her hands and held it, watching and waiting for a response that didn't come. After a couple of minutes, she handed it back to Sara. "I guess he didn't think that was funny," she said, defeated.

"Well, I didn't. I don't get it. Why can't you just say yes when a man asks you out?" Sara asked.

"Let's just finish this up." Rachel said somberly. She was disappointed that Todd didn't text back. Maybe Sara was right. Maybe she was too weird. She probably scared him off. And that was ok. Perhaps God was giving her an out right now, and she should take it.

The two of them finished their color selection and handed them to Johnny with notes for each room. They taped identical chips on the walls for the corresponding rooms. Rachel trusted Johnny, but her philosophy was that it was better to over communicate than leave something to chance. When they finished, Rachel suggested they go to lunch at the deli around the corner. Just as they were leaving, Sara's phone buzzed with a text. Rachel snatched it out of her hands to see the text that came in from Todd's phone. There was a picture of the box along with today's newspaper. The words below read, "No more stalling." Finally, someone who could peak and hold her interest, Rachel thought.

Rachel texted back, "5:45 it is," and handed the phone to Sara. Now she glowed, and she knew it.

Chapter 9

Sunday morning, Rachel attended her regular Baptist church service. She found her mind wandering during the Sunday School hour as those her age spoke about their kids and school. She was 32, and most of the people in her Sunday School class had kids that were pushing middle school. She wasn't married. Or engaged. And she was fine with that; she just got bored listening to their problems because she couldn't relate. She let her thoughts be filled with a replay of Friday night's date with Todd. She wondered if God would approve. The subject of religion had come up briefly on their first date. Todd had mentioned God's grace and used "churchy words" when they spoke about Jesus, but this was the Bible Belt. Rachel knew that many people in the South claimed to be Christians who just went through the motions. She didn't want to be that person. She wanted to be on fire for God's Kingdom. And yet here she sat, in a room full of believers, reading the Word of God, and she was letting the thought of a man get in front of her relationship with God. No wonder Paul spoke about staying unmarried, she thought. This is distracting.

Rachel tried desperately to block the thought of a relationship with Todd out of her mind. She needed to focus on what was important. She listened carefully to the sermon in the worship service, taking notes as the message was delivered and praying for the Holy Spirit to help her concentrate. It was a constant battle throughout the service.

After the service, Rachel went back to her apartment and daydreamed about her date that night. She ate the leftover pizza and started cleaning. Since she was the only occupant, the apartment wasn't difficult to clean, but it took time. She put her headphones in and listened to music as she vacuumed, wondering what would be appropriate to wear on her second date.

Time was passing slowly, but the clock finally turned to 5. She allowed herself to start getting ready. She took another shower and put on navy pants, a cream blouse and 2" heels. She liked the way the outfit showed off her curves but not too much of anything else. She added a silver necklace with a cross on it and pulled out her mother's birthstone ring from her jewelry box. It was a topaz ring set in white gold that Rachel's mother had given to her when she was in college. She wore it on special occasions, or when she wanted to feel pretty. Rachel debated about her hair up or down and decided on down.

She grabbed her keys and purse, and then realized it was only 5:40. She couldn't be early or appear too anxious, although she was. She wondered what Todd had in store for them tonight. Rachel forced herself to stay in the apartment. She paced for 3 more minutes and then couldn't stand it anymore. She locked the door behind her and walked as slowly as she could out the door to the corner of the street where she saw a Todd leaning against the passenger side of his Challenger, parked at the curb.

Todd looked handsome with his khaki slacks and burgundy golf shirt. Both accentuated his muscular physique. He thought about greeting her with a kiss on the cheek, but opted against it. He opened the door for Rachel and held her hand as she entered. He gently closed the door and went back around to his side of the car.

"So, you got me here. Where are we going?" Rachel asked.

"Somewhere special to me. I hope that's alright," Todd replied.

"Fine with me," Rachel replied with a smile, wondering what that cryptic answer meant.

As the Challenger roared down the city streets, Todd started small talk with Rachel, asking about her new business and the construction. Eventually he got around to the box. "I checked out the carving on that box of yours. That's why I wanted to keep it. One of my carving buddies recognized the style. He says it's most likely a design from R.M. Saratoga in Mississippi. Apparently, the man struggled to make a living as a postal worker and then hit it big in his fifties by mistake.

He's got a pretty distinctive style, but this box wasn't one of the ones my buddy has seen. He thinks it is an early work, rumored to be from the lost collection he gave to his daughter for her 8th birthday."

"Why would anyone know that?" Rachel asked.

"I don't know. My buddy watches the biography channel constantly. Probably something he picked up from there," Todd said sarcastically.

"Is it worth anything?" Rachel said.

"My buddy said about $450," Todd answered.

"Why would someone hide a box worth $450 in a wall?" Rachel asked.

"I guess we haven't gotten that far in solving the mystery," Todd said.

"Well, you and I have plenty of other mysteries to focus on – like where are we going?" Rachel asked.

"Oh, you'll see. It's just up ahead," Todd answered with a smile.

The Challenger pulled into the parking lot of Memphis Assembly of God church and parked in the far corner. Rachel's heart raced a bit. Surely, he wasn't taking her to a church service on their second date. And to a "spirit-filled" one? Rachel wasn't sure she was happy about agreeing to go out with Todd again. "What are we doing?" Rachel asked.

Todd gently grabbed her hand with his right hand and clasped his left hand over hers. "We are going to church, and then to dinner if you are up for it. This is part of who I am, so if you and I are going to date, you need to know up front where my priorities are. Just try it, and if you are uncomfortable at all, you say the word, and we'll leave. No questions asked," Todd said.

"Assembly of God," Rachel started, "don't they, um..uh – "

"Speak in tongues? Yeah, sometimes, but not without an interpreter. Look, it's not as intimidating as it seems. I grew up Baptist, so believe me when I tell you, I know what you must be thinking."

"No, I don't think you do," Rachel said. She was thrilled that God was on such a high priority with Todd that he felt it necessary to bring her to church on their second date, but she was very unsure about this particular type of church. She had been taught that speaking in tongues was a dead gift, and that snake oil salesmen used it as a parlor trick to get more people in the doors. She had never known anyone who went to an Assembly of God church.

"You'd be surprised," Todd said with a smile. "Us Baptists are a little uptight when it comes to worshiping. This church just opens up a new dimension of spirituality. Everything in balance, Rachel. Are you ok to try it?"

Rachel was never one to back off a challenge. "Sure, I'm game," she said gripping his hand.

The two excited the vehicle and headed inside. Rachel decided to push aside her presumptions about this denomination of church and have an open mind. It was one service. She could hold out for an hour, right? And if it got really creepy, she'd ask Todd to leave. She was hesitant to hold his hand going into a church service, but she let him lead her by pushing on the small of her back. He kept his arm at a safe distance, only touching slightly to let her know he was there or which way to go. She liked the light touch and was surprised at how comfortable she felt with Todd.

As they entered the church, Rachel didn't see any real differences in layout or composition of the way the church was organized. Someone greeted them at the door, and Todd introduced Rachel right away as his friend. She was glad he didn't say "date". Several other men and women older than her came over and introduced themselves. Everyone seemed friendly and open to her presence. She noticed that no one was overly dressed up or down and there were many different walks of life represented.

As the time for the service to start closed in, Todd led Rachel to a seat in the next to the last row. "Back row Baptist at heart, are you?" she whispered.

He chuckled and said, "Just wanted you to get the full effect without feeling self-conscious about your response. I admit it can be a little different the first time you experience it."

Rachel squirmed in her seat, wondering what was going to happen. She had visions of paralytics rolling down the aisle to be healed and people shouting "Glory Hallelujah" a lot like television evangelist shows. She wondered if someone might pretend to faint during the ceremony only to be healed by the spirit. Rachel chuckled to herself and quickly regained her composure so Todd wouldn't see her poking fun of something he clearly felt was important for her to experience.

As the service started, Rachel was pleasantly surprised by the music, most of which she knew from listening to the local Christian station. She wasn't the greatest singer, so she decided to mouth the words rather than subject Todd to her off-key singing. She saw several people holding their hands up and dancing around, and one lady was crying and praying rather than singing. Rachel felt tears well up, and she was confused. What was this emotion she was feeling? Why was what others were doing affecting her so much? Then she realized that the overflow of emotion from others during worship spoke to her on a different level. These people seemed genuinely engaged in what was going on, and in sharing a communion with God, not in performing for anyone. Suddenly, she felt the spirit of God in the building and His power within herself. She closed her eyes and thanked God for all the blessings in her life and asked him to forgive her for her thoughts about this service. She sang the words to the song out loud and directly to God. She let a tear fall and then caught herself. She quickly pushed the rest back, embarrassed at her own show of emotion. She stopped singing and opened her eyes, looking to see if Todd noticed her, but he was focused on his own worship. And then, as quickly as it came, it was gone. She could no longer feel anything. Rather, she sat and simply watched others throughout the rest of the service. She didn't particularly enjoy the sermon or the rest of the service, but there wasn't anything that went against her own beliefs that was said. The minister had a long altar call, and many people came to the front and knelt at the altar. The minister was overly excited in all his prayers and nearly spit words that began with "p". Rachel was glad to not be sitting in the front row.

She had glanced over at Todd several times during the service to find that he was not paying any attention to her. He had let out several shouts of "Amen" throughout the sermon, and had offered to share his Bible with her during the readings. Other than that, he was laser focused on the worship service. It intrigued Rachel that he was so intense during this time, and she felt a little strange calling this a date. At the conclusion of the service, Todd lightly reached for Rachel's hand. She didn't resist. She laced her fingers in his and studied him as members of the congregation came by to speak to Todd. She could tell he was well-liked in this crowd.

"Hungry?" Todd asked when the crowd subsided.

Rachel smiled and nodded her head. Todd could sense she was a little uncomfortable, and he was ok with that.

49

His philosophy as that sometimes you had to shake things up and see what came loose and what stuck. He hoped Rachel would stick.

Todd lead Rachel out of the building and to the car, making sure to open the door for her as they approached. He climbed in and fired up the engine. He revved it a couple of times as some teenagers walked by because they goaded him. Rachel laughed at his boyish behavior and wondered what was for dinner. Todd left the lot and headed east on Poplar Avenue. Rachel tried to wait for him to start the conversation but couldn't help herself. She finally blurted out, "So what made you choose that church?"

Todd laughed. "You didn't like it, did you?"

Rachel shrugged her shoulders. "It was different; I'll give you that."

"But did you feel anything?" Todd asked.

Rachel wanted to lie, but she couldn't. "Yeah, for a minute."

"That was the presence of God, Rachel. I'm still a Baptist at heart. I just really like being part of a congregation that seeks out the spirit to fill the atmosphere in totality during church. I mean, tell me the last time you had that happen in a Baptist church."

Rachel wanted to protest, but she was having a hard time coming up with an example. Rachel snapped her fingers and pointed at Todd, "Revival. Last year. Calvary Baptist Midtown." Rachel smiled, pleased with herself.

"Last year?" Todd asked.

Rachel scrunched her face. "Yeah, ok, I get it. Well, I don't entirely get it, but I can see the draw."

Todd showed his passion in his response, "I come here to get recharged and to remember that God is everywhere. He is not some foreigner that sits up on high and commands things to happen. He is a real spiritual being who desperately wants to connect with us and have a personal, intimate relationship with you and me."

Rachel was blown away by how deep the conversation had gotten so quickly, and while she wanted to know who he was before she went too far in dating Todd, she wasn't ready to explore all the realms of denominational division on a second date. She liked Todd's interest in a spirit-filled life. She wasn't too sure about speaking in tongues, but for now, she thought she better just speak. And yet nothing came out. Rachel just smiled at Todd and then blurted out, "Me, too." She regretted saying it the instant it left her lips.

"You, what?" Todd asked.

Rachel closed her eyes in embarrassment and tried to cover by telling a half truth, "Want to have a personal, intimate relationship with God." She was telling the truth, but her outburst was directed at Todd. She hoped Todd bought it.

Todd didn't respond, but turned the Challenger into a parking lot that housed several shops and restaurants. "Your pick," he said.

Rachel looked around at the signs. While most of the restaurants appeared to be national chains, she saw one that looked to be an odd ball. "Benny's BBQ," she said decisively.

"Pig it is," Todd replied, pulling the Challenger near the entrance. Rachel had to sit on her hands so she wouldn't open the door before Todd came around. She was a strong, independent woman who ran her own business. Surely, she could handle a car door. But, she played along and found that she enjoyed his efforts.

The restaurant had a fun atmosphere to it, and Rachel soon slipped out of the awkward feel from the conversation in the car about God and the Holy Spirit. She enjoyed her dinner and laughing with Todd about less weighty subjects. He was quick-witted, and Rachel noticed how kind he was to those he encountered. She didn't expect that from a cop. She expected him to be brazen and short with others. His smile lit up the room, and Rachel felt like the only one in it with him at times.

After dinner, Todd drove back to Rachel's apartment complex and parked on the street. He reached into the backseat and handed her the box that he had promised to give back. "I think you held up your end of the bargain," Todd said.

"More than my end if you ask me!" she quipped back, clearly teasing about the church service.

"So, you think I owe you now or something?" Todd replied.

"Maybe," Rachel laughed, purposefully being vague.

Grabbing her hand, Todd walked her in the building. Rachel really enjoyed Todd's company, but she wasn't sure about this whole Assembly of God church he was going to, or the fact that he tried to freak her out on the second date. She liked Todd. He said he wanted to make sure his priorities were understood from the beginning, and while the church might be strange, putting God first was what Rachel longed for in a man. There was more to him than she first imagined. She needed to understand him. She wanted to understand him. But what she really wanted right now was to kiss him.

Rachel stopped at her door and turned around to face Todd, still holding his hand and patiently waiting for him to make a move. He smiled, leaned toward her slowly as Rachel braced for a kiss. Instead, he put his left hand on the door behind her and moved his lips past hers. He whispered in her right ear, "I thought you didn't date cops?"

Frustrated that he didn't just kiss her, Rachel pushed him backwards and said, "Oh, is that what this was? A date?" Her sarcasm was muted by the giggle in her voice.

Todd retreated to a standing position. "Ouch! Well, maybe we should try again. Tuesday?"

"I'll think about it," Rachel said with a sly smile. Todd smiled and slowly turned to walk down the hall. She fumbled her keys and finally turned the knob to open the door. The box slid out of her hands and crashed to the floor. "Todd!"

Chapter 10

"It's all clear. Whoever did this is long gone. Did you make the call?"

"Yes. Who would do this?" Rachel asked, starting to pick up a blouse from the floor.

"Leave it, Rachel."

Rachel mimed popping herself in the head to let Todd know she knew that was a dumb move.

"Try to make a list what's missing, but touch as little as you can," Todd ordered.

Rachel scanned the living room and then the bedroom. "The television is still here."

"It was probably too big to carry. What I can't figure out is how they got in. I don't see any signs of forced entry," Todd said.

Rachel was continuing to look for things that were missing. She was having a hard time coming up with anything. "I can't find anything missing. I guess I don't really have anything valuable," she said.

Todd chuckled, "I wouldn't say that. I would say that you are laying your treasures up in heaven."

"Nice spin," Rachel said as she searched the bedroom. She noticed her jewelry was scattered on the bed. "Hey, Todd, come check this out," she called out.

Todd entered the bedroom to find her sitting on the foot of the bed. "What is it?"

"Most of this is costume jewelry, but these two pieces are real. Why didn't they take them?" She asked, pointing to a sapphire pendant and a white gold necklace.

"Good question. Were they scattered on the bed before the break-in?" Todd asked.

Rachel laughed. "As if! Oh, but I think my jewelry box is missing. Why would someone leave the jewelry and take the jewelry box? It's a Walmart special."

"That is weird. Are you sure it's missing?"

"I think it is," Rachel said as she was looking around the room.

Suddenly, there was a knock on the door. Todd motioned for Rachel to stay put and went to the peep hole to check it out. He opened the door to reveal two uniformed officers. The officers instantly recognized Todd and greeted him with a firm handshake. "Smith. Morgan," Todd said as he tipped his head to them.

"We are here about a break-in?" Morgan asked.

Rachel entered the room. Todd motioned toward her and said, "Guys, meet Rachel Parks. This is her apartment."

Smith extended his arm out to shake her hand. "Ma'am. Sounds like you had some trouble here? Can you tell us what is going on?"

Rachel shook Smith's hand and said, "I came home and found my apartment like this."

"No sign of forced entry that I can see," Todd added, "The building has a key code entry, and the apartment was locked. The windows are sealed shut."

"Are you sure someone was here?" Smith asked reluctantly.

Rachel was offended by the question. "Well, my apartment didn't look ransacked when I left it earlier tonight."

Todd cleared his throat. "What I think Smith meant to say was that we'll look around while Morgan takes your statement."

Morgan pulled out his pen and opened his executive pad revealing blank forms to fill out. "Ok, let's get started. When we are finished, I'll give you a copy, and you can use the police report to contact your insurance company about any missing items," Morgan said.

"But that's just it. There aren't any items that are missing, really. Except for an inexpensive jewelry box," Rachel said.

"Well, let's fill out the paperwork just in case. Sometimes the shock of the event blocks out things. This way if you find something later has gone missing, you'll have a record on file," Morgan said.

Rachel complied with the request to fill out the paperwork while Todd and Smith continued investigating and talking. She couldn't hear their whispers but wondered what they were discussing. They went out into the hallway, and she assumed that was to see if anyone saw anything. Part of the charm of living on the bottom floor was that there were not any neighbors at night and on the weekends. She was surrounded by businesses who were only open Monday through Friday, 8-5. She wondered if the building manager was around and saw anything.

After the forms were filled out, Morgan announced, "Well, that's about all we need tonight. You might want to stay with a friend for a couple of days. Some people find that they have trouble sleeping after a break-in. If we can find any leads or links to other break-ins in the area, we'll be in touch."

Todd and Officer Smith entered the apartment again. Seeing that they were finished, Smith shook Todd's hand again. "Ok, see ya, Man," he said and turned to leave.

Todd tipped his head again and held up his hand, "Thanks, guys," he said as the officers let themselves out of the apartment.

"Rachel, you shouldn't stay here alone tonight. How about your friend Sara? Can you go there?"

Rachel looked at the clock on the stove. It was 11:45. "I'd rather not wake her up. Her husband works the early shift at FedEx. I'll just go to a hotel."

"You should stay with someone tonight," Todd argued. "You never know how this impacts you until the shock wears off."

"I'm a grown woman, ya know," Rachel said, partially offended and partially flattered he cared.

Todd knew all too well that she was very much a grown woman, filled out in all the right places. "You can stay with me," Todd blurted out, almost without thinking.

"No thanks, I'm good. The Motel 6 will leave the light on for me," she chuckled and started picking things up off the floor.

Todd instantly wanted a take-back. He shouldn't have asked that. What was he thinking? He squatted down and met her on the ground, picking up a blouse just before she could get to it. He held it out for her to take and said, "Look, it's not like that."

"I'm perfectly capable of taking care of myself," Rachel said, taking the shirt and putting it away in the bedroom and continuing to straighten her bedroom. Todd felt badly about how his invitation came across and searched for anything to say to convince her his motives were pure. "Look, I'll sleep on the couch, and you can sleep in my bedroom. The door locks from the inside."

Rachel busted out laughing and spun, her eyes meeting his. "The door locks from the inside? That's your pitch? What bedroom door locks from the outside, exactly?"

Todd laughed with her. "I don't know. Look, why don't you pack some things up and think about what you want to do. I've got some calls to make, and then I'll take you wherever you want to go."

Rachel finished straightening her bedroom quickly and grabbed a tote bag from her closet. She stuffed it full of clothes headed to the bathroom. She kept a travel kit packed with toiletries for unexpected client trips, so packing didn't take long. She lugged the tote into the den and continued straightening while Todd completed his phone calls.

After about 45 minutes, she was ready to go, but Todd hadn't returned from the hallway. She wasn't sure if she should interrupt or not, so she sat on the couch for a couple of minutes completely erasing the terror she had felt as she entered her apartment and replacing that emotion with thoughts of what Todd's place must look like. She smiled to herself, but thought it was odd that she seemed unconcerned about the break-in. Then she felt a knot in her stomach. She knew going home with Todd was not a smart choice. She wasn't worried about what Todd might do; she was worried about what she might want him to do. She needed to go to a hotel.

That's where she'd go. And she was perfectly capable of driving herself there, she thought.

Just then, Todd emerged from the hallway holding the box with the angel carving and had a rather concerned look on his face. After seeing Rachel ready to go on the couch he dropped the hand with the box in it to his side, changed his expression and said, "All set?"

Rachel stood up and took a deep breath. "You know what? I think I'm going to go stay with Sara after all."

Todd's expression changed again. This time back to concern. "Look, Rachel, I know I suggested that earlier, but I really think it would be better to keep Sara out of this for now."

"Keep her out of this? What does that mean?"

Todd placed the box gently in the tote Rachel had packed and walked toward her. He put his hands on her shoulders and looked her in the eyes. "Do you trust me, Rachel?"

"Yeah, but – "

"No buts, have I given you any reason not to trust me?"

"Um, I guess not."

"Then trust me when I tell you to come to my house. If you still feel like it is a mistake after we get there, I'll take you wherever you want to go. Deal?"

Rachel could tell that Todd was not trying to charm her anymore. He was serious. Clearly, he knew something he wasn't telling her. "Deal," she said.

Chapter 11

The walk to the Challenger was quick and silent. Todd was holding Rachel's bag in one hand and pulling her with the other. He opened Rachel's door and closed it behind her. He ran around to the driver's side and hopped into the car. He put the car in gear and peeled out of the parking space near the curb. He drove noticeably faster than he had bringing her home, but not too far above the speed limit to concern Rachel. "So, what is it?"

Todd was startled out of thought by her question. "What is what?"

"What is it that you aren't telling me?"

"Is it that obvious?" Todd asked.

"Um, yeah. Like you stopped being my date and went into full-on cop mode," Rachel teased.

"I thought it wasn't a date," Todd smiled.

Rachel smiled back and then squinted her eyes and became serious. "Spill it."

Todd straightened up in his seat. "It's just a hunch, but I think there is a connection between the angel box and your missing jewelry box. I think the thief took your jewelry box by mistake."

"But it's empty. And you said it was only worth about $450. And that's if it is really by that artist guy...what's his name? Saratoga?"

"Yeah, Saratoga. I know this sounds strange, but there is something not right about this whole break-in. The building manager couldn't find your spare key in the office. He had a lot of visitors today delivering packages but nothing out of the ordinary he could put his finger on. With no forced entry, it makes sense that the thief got the key somehow."

"You think my apartment was targeted, not just a random break-in?"

"It was at least premeditated and given that he didn't take things of value, I have to assume he was looking for something pretty specific. Does anyone else know about the angel box?"

"Sara and Johnny - the construction manager - and his crew. They found it in the wall at the house. I just thought some kid left it there –" Rachel stopped herself as she remembered the intruder. "You know, Thursday night I went back to get my phone, and some guy was in the house."

"What? And you didn't call 9-1-1?"

"No, he just ran out when I turned the lights on. There wasn't anything to steal. I just figured it was a squatter or a mischievous teen."

"That's quite a coincidence, Rachel."

"Yeah. Let me guess. You don't believe in coincidences," Rachel said.

"As a matter of fact, I don't," Todd answered.

Rachel squirmed in her seat and started to chew on her nail polish as she stared out the window. She wondered what could be so special about that box that someone would break into her apartment to get it. Staying with Todd didn't seem like such an insanely poor choice anymore.

Chapter 12

Rodney entered the room with a huge smile on his face and almost out of breath. "We got it, Boss."

The gruff man was feeding goldfish in a massive aquarium tank that spanned the length of the wall in his living room. He turned to see Rodney holding a sack. He leaned toward the tank and spoke to the fish, "You hear that, my pretties? We are going to be very rich." He sat the fish food down next to the tank and walked toward Rodney with his hand out. Rodney handed over the sack.

"How did you find it?"

"Shane is buddies with Alfonzo on the construction crew who said they found it in the wall. Gave it to the girl. We just waited until she left her apartment, got the key from the manager's office and searched it," Rodney smiled, proud of himself.

The man dumped the sack out into his hand to reveal a jewelry box with a cross on it. He growled and took a breath before addressing Rodney. The man stuck the box in Rodney's face and yelled, "Tell me what is on the top of this box!"

Rodney was dumbfounded. He stammered and stuttered, "uh – a – uh – a -"

"What is on the top of the box, Rodney?" the man yelled again.

"A – uh – cross," Rodney answered slowly and quietly.

"And what did I tell you was on the box?"

Rodney stood silent, afraid to speak.

"An angel, Rodney. An angel. Not a cross. An angel," the man said using air quotes and sarcasm. "A red dove and an angel. Do you need to write it down?"

Rodney looked at the box and realized it wasn't the right one. "Boss, she has it. We'll make it right."

The man's anger boiled. He threw the box down on the marble floor, and it smashed into a hundred pieces. "You better. And Rodney, this better not come back on me."

Rodney left the room quickly and quietly. He grabbed his phone and made a call. "Give me Shane," he said and waited for an answer. "You got the wrong box! The girl must have it. Where is she?"

"I don't know. We didn't follow her when she left," the voice said.

"Idiots! Find her!" Rodney yelled as he hung up the phone.

Chapter 13

Todd pulled into the short driveway at his house in a suburb just outside of Memphis proper. Rachel noticed his squad car was in the driveway as well. "You get to bring that home?" Rachel asked.

"Oh yeah, it's part of a program they have with Memphis cops and certain neighborhoods with Hud homes. Parking it in the driveway is part of the requirement."

"Interesting," Rachel said. She wanted to know more, but was more interested in finding out what was so special about that box. She opened her door and started to get out. Todd cleared his throat. "Oh, sorry," she said. "Habit."

Todd came around and helped her out of the car. He reached into the back seat and grabbed her bag. They walked up to the house, and Todd opened the door for her. Rachel entered the house, only taking a few steps into the foyer and stopping. It was a quaint house that looked to have been remodeled recently. She noticed the manly looking furniture in the den and huge flat screen television on the wall surrounded by large speakers. Rachel leaned back to see around the corner into the kitchen and then caught herself.

"It's ok, I'll show you around," Todd said. "This is obviously the den. I'll sleep here. To your left is the kitchen. I redid the cabinets and countertops when I moved in."

The sapphire-colored granite countertops were a perfect match to the light oak cabinets. Rachel liked the flat nickel drawer pulls. "Was the tile here when you moved in?"

"Yeah, I got lucky on that. I had to replace the appliances and add the backsplash, though."

"And you knocked that wall out?" Rachel asked, pointing to an area over the sink.

"Yeah, I wanted to open the kitchen up a little more. This way it flows into the eat-in area better."

Rachel liked the upgrades Todd had made. The house was obviously older with a choppier floor plan than her apartment. It looked as if he was handy and had good taste. "Nice," she said.

Todd walked around the corner to a long hallway. "The master is the first door on the left," he said.

Rachel passed him and wondered down the hall. She counted three other rooms with closed doors that she assumed were bedrooms and a bathroom before entering the master bedroom. The hallway was white and could use a touch of color, she thought to herself.

As she entered the master bedroom, she saw masculine decor again, with pictures of muscle cars, a large television hanging on the wall, and a dark blue comforter on a king-sized bed. There were technology chargers all around the room and what looked to be a gun safe in the corner. She was impressed that the bedroom didn't need to be tidied up before she entered. It wasn't like he was expecting company, or was it? Todd entered and placed her tote on the bed. He brushed past her and continued into the master bath. "I'm going to expand this bathroom out the back, but I have to get the permits approved first." Rachel stepped into the bathroom and noticed it was smaller than hers by quite a bit. "Let me just get a couple of things out of here, and then it's all yours," Todd said.

"Sure," Rachel said and walked back into the bedroom to give Todd some space. "What are you going to do when you expand the bathroom?"

Todd yelled around the corner as he grabbed his toiletries, "Make a walk-through shower and double sink vanity."

"Double sink?" Rachel asked, wondering why he needed two sinks.

"Well, I don't plan to be single forever, ya know?" Todd felt awkward saying that out loud to Rachel. He quickly tried to recover, "Plus, it adds value to the house if I decide to sell. The best way to improve your property value is by renovating the kitchen and bath areas."

"Good to know," Rachel replied. She dug in her tote and saw the angel box. She hadn't realized at the time that Todd packed it, but remembered him doing so as she pulled it out. "What do you think is so special about this thing anyway?" she asked Todd.

Todd entered the room with his hands full. "I'm not sure yet," he said, not breaking his stride and continuing to the bath in the hallway. Todd came back to the bedroom door but didn't enter. "I was going to study it tonight and try to see what I could figure out. I'm sure you are tired, but the television works – whatever you want or need, it's yours."

Rachel smiled as she thought to herself, "that's what I'm afraid of," but she didn't utter the words. Instead she asked, "How about a Coke?"

"Sure," Todd said as he went back to the kitchen to grab a can and some glasses with ice. Rachel carried the box to the den and sat on the couch. Todd returned with drinks in hand. He sat Rachel's down on the coffee table in front of her and chose not to sit next to her. Instead he sat on the other, smaller love seat.

Rachel sat up on the edge of the seat and took a sip of Coke. She held the box diagonally and studied the corner that had hit the floor when she dropped it. She started to pick at the corner with her fingers until she pulled enough of the outer shell away to reveal a secret compartment. "Bingo!" she yelled, but she couldn't get into the compartment. She looked at it up close, holding the box 2" from her left eye. "Looks like there is something in there, but I can't get to it," she said as she tossed the box to Todd.

She took a gulp of her Coke while she watched Todd try to open the compartment. He pulled out his pocket knife and tried to use leverage to open it to no avail. He put one hand on top and one hand on bottom of the box and twisted. Nothing. He rotated the box and his hands and tried again, this time having success as the bottom panel moved at a forty-five-degree angle to reveal the hidden compartment. Todd shook the box and an envelope fell out. He inspected the outside of the envelope, shrugged his shoulders and tossed it to Rachel.

"It's an invitation to a wedding from two years ago! Well, I think it's safe to say whoever had this invitation didn't make it to the wedding," Rachel joked. "J.P. Jones and Esther Elizabeth Adams, November 12th. Huh. Wonder what that has to do with our thief. Why would he want an invitation to their wedding?"

"I guess that's our mystery to solve," Todd said.

"Tomorrow," Rachel said with a yawn.

"It is pretty late," Todd said as he stood up.

"Do you really think I'm in danger?"

"Not here," Todd said with a smile as he offered his hand to Rachel. She grabbed his arm and pulled herself off the couch, letting her hand linger on his muscular forearm. After an awkward pause, she stepped away from him, letting her fingers slide down his arm. She grabbed her drink and headed to the kitchen. Todd paused and then followed her.

Rachel emptied the rest of the ice from her drink in the sink and put the glass in the dishwasher. As she turned around, Todd stepped toward her, trapping her against the counter. He leaned toward her, kissed her forehead and then whispered confidently through a smile, "Best second date ever." He didn't wait for a response; he simply turned and walked to the den.

Rachel bit her bottom lip to keep from responding. She smiled as she watched him exit the room. She had to force herself to walk down the hall to the bedroom and not say a word. She entered and shut the door behind her, almost collapsing on the bed. She wanted to text Sara so badly!

Chapter 14

A rat-a-tat-tat knock on the door woke Rachel from a dead sleep. Her eyes popped open. She was disoriented at first. She vaguely remembered her dream, and it definitely had Todd in it. She rolled to the right and saw that the clock read 6:42 am. She let out a small groan as she ran to the door and cracked it ever so slightly to see what was going on. She saw Todd open the front door and heard him whisper, "Shhh!"

An older woman dressed in all brown with lots of costume jewelry and way too much makeup barged in with sacks in both hands. "Ok, what's wrong with my Todd?" Without waiting for an answer, she slammed the sacks down on the floor, pointed her finger in Todd's face, and said, "Jim told me you called him to cover your shift, and I know my Todd never misses a shift, so I rushed right over here and brought you a casserole. It's important to eat when you are sick to keep your strength up."

"No, Ma, I'm not sick. I-"

She interrupted him, "You're not sick? Well what in the Sam Hill was so important that you had to call your brother to cover your shift?"

Todd brought his hand up to his brow and squeezed the bridge of his nose. "Ma – listen-"

"I'm listening." She pulled at Todd's shirt and asked in an accusatory tone, "Did you sleep in your clothes?"

"Yes, ma, I did. Listen." Todd paused for his mother to stop looking at his wrinkled clothes and look at him. He lowered his voice, almost to a whisper, hoping to not wake Rachel. "A friend of mine had an emergency, and I am helping her out, that's all."

"Her? A girl? A girl had some emergency? Oh Todd," she said, rolling her eyes, "you are always taking in strays. What is it this time? Drug addict promising to go straight? Abused wife needed a place to hide out from her big bad husband? I don't know when you will learn that not everyone can be saved."

"But that's just it, Ma. Everyone can be saved, and you know it. That's what God's grace is about."

"Well, you don't have to always be the one to help them find it. You have enough on your plate as it is."

"Ma, keep your voice down. I don't want you to wake Rachel."

"Rachel? That's the floozy's name? Well, I want to wake her up and tell her to get packing. My son is not missing another shift to help some lowlife drug addict pretend to conquer her habit. Where is she anyway?" the woman asked as she walked toward the bedroom.

"Ma!" Todd yelled in his loudest whisper. She spun on her heels, and Todd grabbed the woman gently by her hands. He looked her dead in the eyes and said, "Ma, this girl is not a stray. Someone broke into her apartment last night."

"And you just had to bring her home? She doesn't have any friends or family? Sounds like a stray to me," his mother protested as she pulled from his grip.

"Ma – I like this woman. A lot," Todd said in a loud whisper. "I told you about her – the one from Calvary with the art show for the foster kids?"

"Oh, Rachel!" Todd's mother said loudly, flailing her arms around in the air. "Yes, I remember Rachel. How could I forget Rachel? You go on and on and on about this Rachel every time I see you, but you won't ask her out for some reason." She put her hands on her hips and said in a sassy voice, "Well, you got lucky. I guess fate intervened for you."

"No, Ma, we were on a date when her apartment was broken into. A second date if you have to know."

"Second date? And then you brought her back here? Todd, have I not taught you anything?" his mother said, exacerbated at the thought of what might have occurred overnight.

"Yes, Ma. Nothing happened. I slept on the couch," Todd said as he walked to the couch and grabbed the sheets, pulling them up for his mother to see. "I am a grown man, ya know?"

"Yes, I know. And grown men don't always think before –"

"Ma – nothing happened!" Todd said sending his hands in the air, frustrated with his mother.

Todd's mother grabbed his face with both her hands and pointed it toward her own. She stared at him for a moment as if she could read his thoughts. She saw how much he must like this girl, tilted her head and softened her voice, "You really like her, huh?"

"Yeah, Ma, I do. She's more than I imagined. You'd like her, too."

Tears welled up in his mother's eyes as she smiled proudly at her son. "Well, then, I guess I need to meet her," she said as she dropped her hands from his face and walked past him toward the bedroom. Rachel quickly closed the door and pressed her ear next to it to continue listening.

Todd ran to block her. "Let me see if she's up to company first, ok?"

"Nonsense. I have a casserole. Who doesn't love a good breakfast casserole?" She said out as she tried to push past Todd.

"Ok, Ok," Todd said, touching her shoulders gently to let her know to stay back. "But, Ma - she could be the one, so you have to promise not to scare her off, ok?"

Todd's mom crossed her fingers in an "X" over her chest, smiled, and said, "Cross my heart. I'll be on my best behavior."

Todd walked toward the master bedroom as his mom stayed behind to watch. Todd tapped gently on the door. "Rachel?" he said softly.

Without thinking she answered, "Yeah!" loud enough that he could tell she was next to the door.

"You awake?" he asked, knowing the answer.

Rachel opened the door slightly and poked her head through the crack. "Um, yeah, I'm – I'm awake."

Todd smiled a sheepish grin. "So how much of that did you hear?" he asked.

"Um," Rachel roller her eyes toward the ceiling. "All of it," she said, embarrassed.

Todd put his hands on his hips and closed his eyes as he took a deep breath and let it out loudly. "Well," Todd started as he clapped his hands together, "so I guess you know my mom is here with a casserole, and she'd really like to meet you. You ok with that?"

"Since it's too late to make a great first impression, can I have a couple of minutes to make myself presentable?" Rachel asked in a half chuckle.

"We'll get breakfast on the table. Come out when you are ready." Todd said.

Chapter 15

After taking a very quick, half-cold shower, Rachel dressed in a rush and brushed her hair. She was happy that she had brought work clothes for today. It was Monday, and she planned to work, but more importantly, she wouldn't be seen for the first time by Todd's mother in yoga pants. Meeting Todd's family was not something she had anticipated to ever happen, but especially under these circumstances. She wondered if Todd's mother still thought something happened between them last night. Suddenly, a wave of embarrassment and shame overcame her.

Rachel stood at the door to the master bedroom with her hand on the knob. She could feel her heart racing as she turned it. She took a deep breath, opened the door, forced a smile and walked toward the kitchen.

Todd's mother stood up and walked toward Rachel. "You must be Rachel," Todd's mother said in the politest Southern voice she could muster and the biggest grin possible.

"Yes, ma'am, I am. And you must be Todd's mother?"

The two closed in on one another, and Rachel stuck out her hand for a shake. Todd's mother ignored the outstretched hand and pulled Rachel into a full hug. "You can call me, Jimma," she said, squeezing Rachel tight. "I've heard all about you, dear."

Jimma pulled back from the hug and held her hands on Rachel's shoulder as she looked her up and down. "My, you are a pretty thing. No wonder my boy is so taken with you."

Todd quickly stepped in and pushed his mother aside as he guided Rachel to the table. "Rachel, why don't you have a seat, and we'll have some breakfast. Momma makes the best breakfast casserole this side of the Mississippi."

"Yes, I do and don't you forget it," she said. "The secret is in the sausage. You can't buy that bargain brand stuff and expect the casserole to come out right."

"Sounds lovely, Ms. Jimma," Rachel said with a smile as she sat down.

"Oh, honey child, it's not Ms. Jimma, just Jimma. See, when my oldest son was a boy, he had a friend who used to tell everyone in the neighborhood I was Jim's ma, only he had a lazy tongue, and it came out Jim ma. After a while, it just stuck that I was Jimma. Everyone calls me that now. My real name is Ima Gene, but I never much cared for that anyway. So Jimma it is."

Todd served the casserole. "Ma is the treasurer at the country club and president of the WMU down at

Hickory Grove Baptist," Todd said, trying to fill in the conversation.

"Three years running," Jimma said with a smile.

Rachel said, "I think my church runs some cooperative campaigns with you through the Shelby County Association, maybe for battered women?"

"Yes, I think you are right. You belong to Calvary Baptist, don't ya, honey?" Jimma asked, knowing the answer.

Rachel was almost surprised she knew what church, but then remembered the conversation she overheard. Apparently, Todd had spoken to his mother about her many times. "Oh, yes, ma'am. I've been there for a while. I teach an art class on Thursdays during school and work on foster programs. I also sing in the choir, but not because I'm any good. They will let anyone make a joyful noise," Rachel giggled. Jimma smiled.

"Ma, Rachel owns her own advertising agency in midtown," Todd said.

"Oh, how lovely. I've always said this town could use more women in business. Good for you, darlin'."

Rachel took a bite of the casserole. "This is marvelous, Jimma. I think you are right about that sausage."

"Darn Skippy," Jimma said. "Now I heard you had some trouble at your apartment last night, and my boy was there to help. Are you ok, sweetie?"

Todd interrupted. "Ma, I don't think Rachel wants to talk about it."

"No, it's fine, Todd." Rachel said, trying to make a good impression on his mother. "Yes, ma'am, someone broke into my apartment last night while we were at dinner. Todd graciously let me stay in his house overnight. I didn't want to intrude, but he thinks I might be in danger." She paused to look at Todd and smile, "You know, I can see where your son gets his good manners from. He's a good host."

"Not too good, I hope," Jimma said with a wink to Rachel who instantly looked down at her plate, embarrassed by the implication.

"Ma!" Todd said and shot her a shocked and evil look.

Rachel thought she deserved that one and let it slide.

"Oh honey, we are all adults here. I can see Rachel here is a fine, upstanding young woman. You wouldn't deny your mother a little fun, now would you?" Jimma took another bite of her casserole. Todd shot her another look of disapproval.

Rachel suddenly had an idea. "Jimma, have you heard of a J.P. Jones or an Esther Elizabeth Adams?"

"Why do you ask?" Jimma said.

"There were married a couple of years ago at the Country Club." Rachel ran to get the invitation and showed it to Jimma. "I thought you might could tell us about it."

Jimma looked at it closely as Rachel sat back down. "Oh yes, I remember this couple. It was a huge scandal at the club – the wedding that never happened. The ladies loved all the gossip they got out of this wedding. She came from old money here in town, and he was some sort of salesman. Rumor was that they had a huge fight in front of a bunch of people in Tunica a week before the big day, and he threw her off the ship. They never found her body, though."

Rachel was shocked at the information that Jimma provided. "He killed her?"

"Well, that was the scuttlebutt anyway. No one knows for sure. Her momma died of a broken heart after being so embarrassed by what had happened and saddened by her daughter's death. Poor thing."

"Who was her mother?" Rachel asked.

"Mary Adams. She used to live on Oak Trail in midtown. She was a strange woman, though. I never much cared for her. Her family had money from selling art or something, but she didn't care much for those of us who worked for our money – like your daddy, bless his soul."

Rachel and Todd tried to process what Jimma told them. "Oak Trail. Are you sure, Ma?" Todd asked.

"Yes, I'm sure of it. Why?" Jimma asked.

Todd's eyes locked with Rachel's. "Ma, I don't want to be rude, but we gotta go."

84

Todd and Rachel got up from the table as Jimma said, "Oh don't mind me. It's not like I was planning to spend the day with my son or anything."

Todd leaned down and kissed Jimma on the forehead. "I'm sorry, Ma. I'll catch up with you later, I promise."

Jimma could sense the seriousness in his tone. "Yeah, yeah. Go. Get out of here. I'll clean this up."

Chapter 16

Todd and Rachel met up in the den. "That's got to be my house!" Rachel said.

"I know. Look, we have a lot of work to do, but you need to clear your day so we can get this moving. Can you do that?" Todd asked.

"Yeah, give me a few minutes. Fortunately, I had cleared a lot of my schedule to manage Johnny's work at the house. But I've worked with him a long time, so I can trust him to do the work right. Do you think it's safe for them to be there?" Rachel said.

"Yeah, I would just alert them to the intruder the other night. I'll have patrol step up the rounds and focus on the house for the next few days." Todd answered. "I'm going to take a shower and my change clothes before we get going."

"What about your schedule?"

"Jimmy's got my shift today, remember? I'm good." Todd had a nagging feeling about the encounter with his mother and knew he needed to correct the situation. He walked over to Jimma and spoke quietly to her while she cleared the table.

Rachel couldn't hear his side of the conversation, but Jimma didn't know how to be quiet. After Todd spoke for a while, she smiled, hugged Todd and said, "Oh, sweetie. I thought you'd never ask! Of course, of course!"

Todd finished hugging his mother and retreated to the bedroom. Rachel noticed Todd's Bible was laid out on the table and opened to Isaiah. He had marked in it quite a bit. Rachel smiled and then got busy on her phone and iPad. She called Johnny first to let him know that he should watch out for anything unusual and that the police would be stepping up patrols. Then she sent eight emails to different clients providing updates so she wouldn't be disturbed and dialed Sara's number. She didn't know how much she should share, but she had to warn Sara not to go to the house alone and to let her know she would be out of pocket at least today.

Sara answered on the first ring. "Well, you are up early, that doesn't bode well for your date, huh?" Sara said, disappointed and fishing for gossip.

Rachel was a little thrown off and replied, "What? No, it's fine. Listen, that's not why I'm calling. I'm going to be tied up today. Can you get the photos from Richard for our photo shoot and load them on the server?"

"Yes, but only if you give me the scoop on your date with hottie McCop?" Sara said through laughter.

"I can't now, Sara. I need to talk to you about work. What is on your plate today?"

"I'm still working on copy for the Marshall ad campaign, and I have three interviews with potential candidates today at the office –

"New or old?" Rachel interrupted.

"Old. Duh, we don't have any furniture at the new one yet, remember?"

"Great. Listen, Johnny is painting today so steer clear of there for a couple of days, ok?"

"Yeah, whatever – I'm so not interested in going there until his crew is finished, and the bugs are gone. That's your project anyway. So, did you finally kiss him?"

"Focus, Sara," Rachel said in a huff. "If Sam calls, text me, but other than that, it's going to have to wait, ok?"

"Fine. But you have to give me something. I'm dying to know about your date!" Sara said.

Rachel took a breath and decided she needed to be sensitive to Sara's needs. None of this was Sara's fault, and she just wanted to see her friend happy. Rachel smiled and turned away from the kitchen, just in case Todd's mother could hear. "It was great, Sara."

Sara squealed in the phone so loud Rachel had to pull it away from her ear. She looked back to see if Todd's mother was listening but didn't see her. "And is he a good kisser? Oh, I bet he is a good kisser!" Sara asked.

88

"I'll have to let you know about that when it happens," Rachel said.

"What? You still haven't kissed him?" Sara shrieked in disbelief.

"Not yet, but I'm pretty sure I will soon."

"Oh, darn, my other phone is ringing. Gotta go, but text me some details, ok?"

"Later." Rachel said and hung up the phone. She was pleased that conversation went so well. Sara seemed so focused on her date with Todd that she didn't even question what was going on.

Rachel opened her iPad back up and banged out a couple of other emails, moving meetings set for tomorrow into the following week, just in case. Jimma entered the den with her bags clanging and startled Rachel.

Jimma reached down to hug Rachel, awkwardly with her hands full. "Oh, honey, I didn't mean to sneak up on you or anything. I've got to get going. I can't trust those ladies at the church to do any work unless I'm there; all they want to do these days is gossip"

Rachel let her iPad slide off her leg as she awkwardly hugged Jimma back. "It was so nice to meet you, Jimma."

"You, too, honey," Jimma said with a huge grin. She backed away from Rachel and headed to the door.

"Oh, let me get that for you, Jimma," Rachel said as she sprang into action to open the door. "Thank you for the breakfast this morning. It was world-class!"

Jimma smiled and said, "My pleasure," as she left the house. She hollered over her shoulder on the way to her car, "Listen, you tell Todd I'll see y'all later tonight, ok, sweetie?"

"Ok, Jimma. Bye" Rachel waved and wondered if she really meant that or if that was just her Southern hospitality coming out.

"Did I hear my momma leave?" Todd asked as he emerged from the bedroom dressed in tactical pants and a black t-shirt, weapon holstered on his hip. Rachel noticed that he looked even better in tactical gear than his uniform.

"Yeah, you just missed her. But she said something about seeing you tonight?"

"Listen, I'm sorry about all that. My mother can be a little pushy at times. I'll make it up to you."

"I'm counting on it. Hey, I found that Mary Adams was the owner of my new house before the sale, so we are on the right trail."

"How did you do that?" Todd asked, impressed.

"I'd love to tell you I'm just that smart, but really the internet is a powerful place for public records. It wasn't too difficult."

Todd chuckled. "Ok, well, let's head to the precinct first. I might can top your intel with some higher-powered searches. You ready?"

"Let me grab my bag," Rachel said as she picked up her phone, iPad, the angel box and invitation and ran to the master bedroom. She stuffed everything in the tote and headed back to the den. "Ok, now I'm ready."

As they approached the Challenger, Todd rounded the front of the car to open the door for Rachel. Rachel pushed the door closed and stepped toward Todd. "We need to talk first."

Todd let his hand slide off the handle and backed up. "Ok?"

"I really like the way you treat me like a lady, I really do. I like you opening doors for me, and I don't want you to stop, but today, we may not have time for all that. Today – just today, I need to be your partner and open my own door. Ok?"

Todd was stunned by her request. He smiled and chuckled. "Just for today?"

"Yes, just for today. Or until we finish this. And then you can go back to being this great Southern gentleman, ok?"

"Hmmm. A lady partner. This could be interesting," he chided. Rachel wrinkled her nose and smirked. "Ok, ok, I can do that. But I have something I need you to do for me," Todd started.

"Ok, sure," Rachel answered, "What is that?"

"I need you to forgive me."

"For what? We've already covered your mom. I like her. It's totally fine."

"No, it's not. Listen, the enemy comes to steal, kill and destroy, and if we don't protect ourselves from him, we invite him in."

"What are you talking about?"

"I shouldn't have asked you to come to my house last night."

"Oh, I'm so sorry. I shouldn't have intruded. Your mom -I -"

Todd interrupted, "No, that's not it." Rachel looked confused. Todd paused to collect his thoughts. "Paul tells us to flee temptation, not to fight it. That's a difficult stance for me, especially in my line of work. And in my pride, I chose to fight rather than flee, which meant I put you in a precarious situation with your reputation. I'm asking you to forgive me for that, and to know that I will work hard to not only restore it but to not put you in that situation ever again."

Rachel was speechless. She tried to process what Todd just said. "I think you might have to run that by me again."

Todd tried again. "Rachel, I don't think it's a secret that really like you. And although nothing happened last

92

night, I should have found another option. I was playing with fire because I like the rush. But it wasn't right to put you in a situation where there was even a possibility someone could have misinterpreted what was going on."

"I'm a big girl, Todd. We're good." Rachel said, still not completely sure what he meant.

Todd was satisfied with her answer and got into the car. They rode in silence to the precinct as Rachel played his words over and over in her head. Flee from temptation, precarious situation, restore her reputation? She wondered who talked like that. Clearly, he was concerned about the scene with his mother and the effect that had on her. He was protecting her. She didn't really understand the fleeing part, but one thing was certain. Todd liked her. And she liked him.

Chapter 17

Todd pulled the Challenger in to a parking spot at the precinct and looked over at Rachel. "Don't listen to anything anyone says in here, ok? Especially Marcus."

Rachel smiled. She liked the thought that Todd must have spoken about her to his friends at the police station. She exited the vehicle and followed Todd to the door. He held it open out of habit. As they entered several officers greeted him but continued with their work. Todd walked over to a desk and started to speak with the officer behind it when Marcus interrupted.

Marcus was a slender and tall police officer, mid-20s with a huge smile. "Hey, Todd. Are you not going to introduce us to this fine-looking woman?" Marcus started and then turned to Rachel and said in a lower voice covering his mouth with his hand as if it were a secret, "This guy is no gentleman. I wouldn't be seen with him if I were you."

"Is that right?" Rachel said, playing along.

"Hey, Marcus. Rachel, this is Marcus – remember I told you about him?" Todd said.

"You told her about me already? Thanks, brother," Marcus said to Todd and then turned to Rachel. "Did he tell you I was single? Because you and I could have a whole lot –"

"Marcus!" Todd said with a condescending tone. He turned to Rachel, "Don't mind Marcus. He was just leaving." Todd turned his glare back to Marcus.

Marcus stepped back. "I'm hurt, brother. I am genuinely hurt."

"Well, go be hurt over there, man," Todd chided.

Marcus walked backward away from them, held up his arm to point at Rachel and mouthed, "Me and you."

Todd shot Marcus another look. Marcus held both hands up and turned to walk away.

Todd finished his business with the man behind the desk and led Rachel down the hall. "We can use the computer at Echols' desk." As they approached the desk, Todd pulled the rolling chair out for Rachel and grabbed a nearby stationary one for himself. He quickly logged into the computer and pulled up screens Rachel didn't know what they were. Todd typed away and clicked at what looked like random pages to Rachel.

"What are we looking for?" Rachel asked.

"A thread to pull," Todd said.

"Oh," Rachel responded, clearly annoyed at being left out of the search. "Well, while you are doing that, I think I'll search on my own, ok?" Rachel said as she pulled out her iPad.

"Sure, two heads are better than one," Todd said back.

Rachel started punching in different search terms while Todd did his thing. He picked up the phone, made calls, typed in different things. Rachel wondered what type of thread he was looking for exactly. After some time, she managed to locate the obituary for Mary Adams in the Commercial Appeal. "Hey, Mary Adams has a son, Martin Schuler Adams. Says here he lives – or lived in – Braden, Tennessee."

Todd was on the phone and held one finger up to indicate he was busy. After he hung up he wrote a note down and said, "Our friend J.P. was just released from prison last week."

"What? From killing his fiancé?"

"Well, they only had circumstantial evidence. He took a deal. 18 months is all he served. I need to go talk to his parole officer to find out anymore."

"Then I guess we have our thread to pull," Rachel smiled.

Chapter 18

Todd and Rachel entered the plain brown building looking for J.P. Jones' parole officer. Rachel immediately went to the directory. "What's his name?" she asked.

"Railey, Doug Railey."

"Room 104," Rachel said as they headed down the hall.

The room was on the left next to the restrooms, and the door was ajar. Todd knocked on the door and peered his head around the corner. The officer didn't look up. "Yes?" he asked.

"Doug Railey?" Todd asked with Rachel standing just out of site to his left.

"You betcha. And you?" The older gentleman said looking up from his paperwork and over the black-rimmed reading glasses on his nose.

"Todd Henderson, Memphis, second precinct," Todd said as he flashed his badge from under his black t-shirt.

"What can I do for you, Officer Henderson?" Doug said, skeptical.

As he entered the room, Todd motioned for Rachel to stand in the hallway. "I'm looking for information about one of your parolees, a J.P. Jones."

"Yes, he's one of mine. What are you needing?" Doug asked.

"His file says the original charges were for murdering his fiancé, but since there was no body, he took a deal. I wonder if you can tell me anything about why he might do that or anything else about him," Todd asked eagerly.

"I don't really judge those who have agreed to pay a debt to society. My job is to help them once they are out – you know, make sure they stay on the straight and narrow." Doug paused and stared at Todd for a minute. "Is this related to some case you are working? It might be more productive for you to tell me what you are working on."

Todd looked down, not sure what he should share or what information he really hoped the parole officer could provide. "I'm investigating a link between J.P. Jones and the house that belonged to his fiancé's mother."

"What sort of link?" Doug asked.

Frustrated, Todd said, "Well, that's what I'm trying to establish. Anything you can tell me about him – why he wanted to marry Esther, why he might have tried to kill her, where he lives or what he's doing now - anything at all would be helpful."

Yanking his reading glasses off his face and slamming them onto the desk, Doug asked, "Is this official police business, son?"

Todd couldn't lie. "Not exactly. Well, it might be if I can find a connection between your parolee and a burglary."

"You know you need to be on official police business for me to discuss this with you, right?" Doug asked.

"Yes, sir, I do. It is a case in my precinct, but it's not a high priority for them. I believe there is more to it than meets the eye." Todd answered.

"I'm sorry son, I can't help you," Doug answered, picked up his glasses and went back to his paperwork.

Todd stood up and motioned for Rachel to come in. "Mr. Railey, meet Rachel Parks. She bought the house that belonged to Ether Adams' mother. Recently, the house and Rachel's apartment were burglarized. I think the two break-ins are related and that because the thief has not found what he was looking for, he will be back. Now you and I both know that the police can't protect her against what might happen, especially if they don't know what that is. I do know for certain there is a link to J.P. Jones and his fiancé; I just don't know what it is." Doug stopped writing and looked up at Todd. "Please, sir."

"Son, I can see you care about this woman and really believe she might be in danger. But I can't really divulge anything about Mr. Jones unless there is a crime committed or you have official business. I can tell you what is public knowledge. Mr. Jones was indeed charged with the murder of his fiancé, Ether Adams, whose body was not recovered, and he took a plea deal with the D.A."

Rachel interjected, "Why would he take a plea deal if there was no body? Wouldn't that tell the jury there is reasonable doubt that she's even dead?"

Doug smiled. "Why, yes, I would think so, Ms. Parks."

Rachel placed her hands on the desk and leaned forward. "So why would he do that?" she asked.

Doug looked at Rachel carefully. He paused and smiled back at her. Finally, he lowered his voice and said, "Far be it for me to judge a man's intentions, but in my experience, a man who makes a deal like that has other skeletons in his closet that he needs to keep hidden, if you know what I mean."

Rachel locked eyes with the man and smiled as big as she could. "Like certain connections?"

"Like certain connections," Doug confirmed with a smile as he sat back in his chair.

Todd stepped forward and asked, "And if a man such as Mr. Jones were to need to protect his connections, can you tell us what type of business might he specialize in?"

"Oh, I really couldn't say," Doug answered.

"But you might could take a guess," Todd said. Doug frowned and crunched his body back over his desk.

"Hypothetically, of course," Rachel said.

"Hypothetically, I wouldn't know," Doug said as he shuffled papers on his desk. He looked up again over his glasses and said, "I really do wish you all the best. Now if you will excuse me, I need to mail some letters," taking special care to enunciate the words "mail some letters."

Todd and Rachel left the room and headed for the car. Rachel blurted out as soon as they got into the car, "Did that guy really just tell us that J.P. Jones went to jail to protect his business connections? Who does that? The mob?"

"Rachel!" Todd reached to grab her hand. "He's just an old man who needs some excitement in his life. Think about it – he sits there all day talking to these ex-cons and pushing paperwork. He's probably pulling our legs to get a rise out of us. For all we know, this guy is dumb as a box of rocks and didn't think about the fact that there wasn't a body. He may have thought the police had enough evidence to put him away for life, especially if he's guilty. Let's follow the threads one at a time and see where they lead," Todd said, trying to comfort her.

"You're right," Rachel said, much more confident after Todd's firm touch.

"Want to grab some lunch?" Todd asked.

"I thought you'd never ask!" Rachel said.

Chapter 19

Lunch was at a hole-in-the-wall local diner restaurant in Tunica, just down the street from the big casinos. The building was an old barn that had been converted into a restaurant. The roof was a blue tin, something that must make great noise in the rain, Rachel thought. The sign read, "Roger's." It was quaint and folksy, and everyone in the place greeted you with a smile and a "how ya doin', honey?" Rachel especially enjoyed all the pictures on the wall from celebrity visitors. She didn't think the food was all that note-worthy, but she could see the pride these people obviously had in their work.

"Tell me about your dream," Todd said out of the blue.

"My what?" Rachel asked, nearly choking on a biscuit. How did he know?

"Your new business," Todd said.

"Oh, yeah, my dream," Rachel started. "I guess it's silly, really, but I've just always wanted to work in advertising. I used to make these crazy recordings when I was a child, pretending to sell chewing gum or a Barbie doll. I always thought it would be fascinating to come up with those campaigns."

"You used to make your own commercials?" Todd asked with a smile, clearly enjoying her.

"Oh yeah. I was all in, too. I'd make a television campaign with the camcorder, complete with posters and props and everything. I was such a nerd!" Rachel laughed.

"I bet you were something," Todd said. Todd was mesmerized by her smile and her passion.

"Oh yeah. I used to drive my mom crazy, making her watch them over and over and over. There was this one I did about chocoholics anonymous. I'm not sure what I was proposing to sell, exactly, but I remember doing a bit where I bent over and stuffed my face full of chocolate."

"I'd really like to see those!" Todd joked.

"Not going to happen!" Rachel laughed. "I think I'm better behind the camera than in front of it these days."

"Not from where I'm sitting," Todd said as he reached for her hand. They smiled and shared a moment. "So why the new place?"

"Oh, Sara and I do pretty well on consulting, but I've always wanted a full-service agency. We can't do it all and service our clients fully without a larger staff. I found the house by accident. It was such a good price that I convinced Sara to go in with me, and then the whole thing just started unfolding from there. I've talked to our current client base about expanding, so I think we have a good business plan moving forward. I just need to land a couple of big -" Rachel realized she had been going on and on about her and suddenly stopped. "I'm sorry. This probably sounds incredibly boring and trite to someone who saves lives for a living."

"Rachel – no, I do what I do so you can do what you do," Todd said.

"Really?" Rachel said, not convinced. "Tell me why you are a cop."

"My dad was a cop. My brother is a cop."

Rachel thought for a minute, "And you never thought of doing anything else?"

"I don't know. It's really all I've ever known. While you were making commercials as a kid, I was riding around in the cruiser with my dad, pretending to answer calls on the radio or going shooting with him at the range. Being a cop was just expected I guess."

"And now? If you had a choice to do it over, would you do something different?" Rachel asked.

"That's the thing about life. You don't get a lot of do-overs. I'm a cop."

Rachel looked down at her plate and felt the weight of that statement. She was dating a cop. And one that didn't seem to want to change. Before this went too far, she needed to be honest with herself and Todd about her feelings.

"Todd, I –um, I," she started as Todd sensed the tension in her voice.

"Don't date cops," Todd he finished.

"Right," Rachel said softly, looking down at her plate. "It's just that – "

"Rachel, you don't have to explain. A lot of women are uncomfortable with my profession. It comes with the territory." Todd felt the need to break the tension. "I think they can't handle all the raw power in these biceps!" Todd said as he flexed his muscles and smiled.

He was charming, Rachel thought. "I think I could take you," Rachel said, flirting with him.

"Oh yeah, you think so? Let's go then. Come on," Todd said as he put his hand out ready to arm wrestle Rachel on the table.

Rachel played along. She moved the plates to the side of the table out of their way and grabbed his right hand with hers.

"Ready? Go!" Todd said as he barely tensed his hand.

Rachel stood up quickly and put both her hands on his right hand, using leverage to push his arm down. Todd reacted fast. He tensed up his muscles and pulled Rachel around the table and onto his lap. "I think I won that round," he said with a laugh.

Frustrated, Rachel said, "I think you cheated is what you did."

"Cheated? What? I am not the one that used two hands and stood up!" Todd protested with a huge grin.

"I said I could take you. Not that I could beat you arm wrestling," Rachel flirted back.

"Ah, I see now, that's much different," Todd said as he helped her up. "Come on, let's go."

As they entered the car, Todd pulled out his phone and punched in letters. As he waited for it to load, Rachel asked, "Where to now?"

"I want to stop by J.P.'s lawyer's office," Todd said.

"His lawyer? Isn't he just going to give us the old, 'attorney-client privilege' speech?" Rachel asked.

"Probably. But you always have to try to pull the thread," Todd said.

Chapter 20

Rachel reached for the air conditioner vent and turned it toward her as they sped down the road. She thought about what the parole officer had told them. She wondered what business J.P. was into and if he really did want to protect connections. It seemed like a steep price to pay. There must have been a reward coming for him to do that, she thought to herself.

As they approached the building, Rachel's phone buzzed. It was Sara. "Sam wants the drawings tomorrow am in his office," the text read.

"Ok, thanks," Rachel replied.

"Everything ok?" Todd asked.

"Yeah, I just have to take care of a needy client tomorrow," Rachel said with a smile.

"Ok, let's see what we can wrap up, then," Todd said as he exited the vehicle.

As they entered the building, the receptionist greeted them. She was a large woman with brown hair and brown eyes. She looked to be in her late 40s and had nails longer than Rachel had seen in quite some time.

She was wearing a V-neck top that was showing a little too much. "May I help you?" she said through a bubble in her chewing gum. As she looked up, the bubble popped on her face, and she stared at Todd, clearly enjoying looking at him.

"Um, Lance Robertson, please," Todd said, flashing his badge.

"You got an appointment, honey?" The receptionist asked.

"No, ma'am. I just need to see Lance about a case. Won't take but a minute of his time," Todd answered. He noticed her staring and leaned his arm on the desk. He smiled at her and winked. "If you could help me out, I'd really appreciate it," he whispered.

The receptionist clearly liked his flirting. She grabbed his arm and giggled. "Let me see what I can do." She came out from behind the desk and started walking quickly to a room to the left of the reception office. Her jewelry jingled with every step, and Rachel wondered if she was going to come out of those 5" black stiletto heels or turn an ankle. She was gone less than a minute. When she returned, she came around from behind the desk to greet Todd face to face. "He said he'd see you in a few minutes. You can have a seat." She squeezed his bicep and smiled. "If you need anything else, you let me know," she said as she stared into his brown eyes and giggled.

"Thank you," Todd winked at her as he pulled Rachel to sit down.

Rachel was unamused but didn't say anything. Instead, she pulled out her phone and began banging out emails, taking care of business that had come in the past couple of hours. She called Johnny to check on construction progress, and he told her they were painting and all was well. Rachel picked up a magazine. She pretended to read while keeping one eye on the receptionist who was watering plants in the office, Rachel thought mostly to find an excuse to get near Todd.

Finally, the receptionist ended her watering task and returned to her desk, just in time to answer a ringing phone. "He'll see you now," she said. "First door to the left."

The office was much larger than Rachel had imagined given the outside of the building. The walls were lined with beautiful art. The center of the room hosted a 4-top table, and Rachel noticed a putter and portable green to the left of the desk as well as a bookshelf full of collectible items behind her. "Mr. Robertson?" Todd asked extending his hand.

"And you are?" Lance asked. He was dressed in a double-breasted blue silk suit with light pinstripes and a white button-down shirt. His shoes were polished and his tie perfectly straight. His hair was gray and slicked back. He had a Southern drawl to his voice, and he spoke slowly.

"Todd Henderson, Memphis PD, second precinct," Todd said as he flashed his badge.

"What can I do for you today, officer?" Lance asked, closing the door and showing the two to the table in the center of the room.

Rachel and Todd sat down. Todd waited for Lance to approach the table before he started. "I'm working a case, and I found a link to a previous case of yours. I was hoping you'd shed some light on it for me."

"I'll do what I can, within the law, of course." Lance said as he sat down, "What's the case?"

"J.P. Jones," Todd asked, watching for a reaction.

Lance didn't seem bothered by the suggestion. "Doesn't ring a bell. And you think I defended him?"

"Yes, according to the court records, you were his attorney. His fiancé was murdered, but they didn't find the body," Todd answered.

"Hmmm, now let me think. Oh yes, I remember now. The case with the missing body," Lance offered, completely unemotional. "At the casinos, right?"

"Yes, that's it," Todd said. "Can you tell us why Mr. Jones took the deal?"

"Well, I'd imagine because he didn't want the death penalty, officer, Henderson, was it?" Lance offered.

"But there was no body. Was he really going to be convicted without a body?" Rachel blurted out.

"Well, Miss -?"

"Parks," Rachel answered but didn't give any further information.

"Well, Miss Parks, as I'm sure you are aware, juries can be quite unpredictable," Lance answered.

"Is that what you advised Mr. Jones?" Todd asked. "That he should take a deal in case the jury is unpredictable?"

"What exactly are you getting at, officer?" Lance asked.

"I'm just trying to establish if you think there is any other reason why he would take that deal?"

"I wouldn't know what motivates a man such as J.P. Jones to take a deal," Lance said.

"But surely you had an opinion that you shared with Mr. Jones." Todd said.

"Is that a statement or a question, officer?" Lance said, defensively.

"I'm just wondering as his attorney, why would you let him take a deal if there was reasonable doubt," Todd said.

"I'm obligated as a member of the bar to present all deals to my client and advise him of his options."

Todd could feel the conversation spiraling out of control and knew that Mr. Robertson was not going to break privilege. "Of course, of course. Do you know if Mr.

Jones was concerned at all about his personal life coming out in court?"

Lance relaxed in his chair and said, "I would imagine all my clients are concerned about that. Mr. Jones would be no different."

Todd stood up and walked to the bookshelf. He picked up a glass case with an autographed baseball in it. "You don't seem like the appointed attorney type."

Lance chuckled. "Hardly."

Todd put the baseball case down and wondered where J.P. got his money. "What was it that J.P. did for a living?"

"I couldn't say, privileged information and all," Lance said with a smile. "You know, the reporters were relentless in digging, but after he took a deal, they seemed to drop the whole story."

"Is there anything you can tell us that struck you as odd or out of the ordinary about this case?" Todd asked.

"That I'm at liberty to say? I don't think so," Lance said with a smirk.

Todd stood up and held out his hand. Rachel stood as well. "Thank you for your time, Mr. Robertson," Todd said.

Lance stood, shook Todd's hand and put his left hand on Todd's shoulder. He guided Todd out of the office and waved. "Always happy to help the police out," he said.

Todd winked at the receptionist as they left. Rachel rolled her eyes, and as soon as they were outside the building she started wiping her arms. "What are you doing?" Todd asked.

"Oh, I can just feel the slime sticking to me," Rachel said.

Todd laughed. "He does ooze it, doesn't he?"

"And you! What was with you and that receptionist?" Rachel said, disgusted at the thought.

Todd laughed and said, "Ah, pumpkin, are you jealous?"

"As if!" Rachel said in a huff. "I just can't believe you would flirt with her to get to see that lawyer."

Todd laughed, "Yeah, because you didn't use any charm with Mr. Railey to get information."

Rachel squinted her nose up in frustration. "That was different," Rachel said, knowing it wasn't. She huffed as she got into the car, yanking her seatbelt across to buckle it and fumbling with her phone and purse, trying to find something to do to distract herself from Todd.

Todd smiled and climbed in the car, pleased that Rachel seemed jealous and that he had riled her up. They rode in silence for a few miles as Rachel banged on her iphone. Todd wasn't sure if she was actually working or just trying to pretend until she could calm down. He thought it was nice because it meant she liked him. He enjoyed the drive, daydreaming about spending time with Rachel after the mystery was solved and she was no longer in danger. He hoped she would change her mind about dating a cop.

Chapter 21

About 15 minutes into the ride, Todd's phone rang. Rachel stopped what she was doing long enough to try to eavesdrop. She could only hear Todd's side of the conversation, which consisted of "yes sirs" and "no sirs". After he hung up, she asked, "Everything ok?"

"Yeah, I just have to take care of a needy captain tomorrow," Todd said back with a smile.

Rachel instantly got the reference to her call from earlier. "I guess we both have work to do tomorrow."

The rest of the trip was relatively quiet. Rachel's mind was racing back and forth between the mystery of the angel box, J.P. Jones and of course, that odd conversation with Todd. She enjoyed thinking about Todd more and let her mind linger on thoughts of him. She knew she needed to end this – whatever this was – before it was too late. She didn't need to get involved. She didn't want to hurt Todd, but, more importantly, she didn't want to be hurt. She had seen way too much of that in her life. She stared out the window, taking in the flat landscape as the wheels turned.

As they approached Memphis, Rachel noticed they were going away from Todd's house. "Where are we going?" She asked.

"Oh, I thought you might want a few things before we head out to Collierville," Todd said as he turned onto Tennessee Street.

"Collierville?" Rachel asked, with her nose crinkled. "What's in Collierville?"

"Dinner," Todd said.

Todd's vagueness drove Rachel crazy, in a good sort of way. She liked surprises, but he just seemed incapable of coherent speech sometimes. Well, most men in her opinion struggled with effective communication, and she didn't figure a cop would have a leg up on most men. Or maybe, he just liked pushing her buttons. It did seem to be their thing. Suddenly, Rachel was self-conscious. Maybe she needed to change or take a shower before going wherever it was Todd was taking her. She wondered what was in her closet that would be appropriate, but she chose not to ask for more details. A surprise would be nice after the past 24 hours, she thought.

Todd pulled up to the curb just outside her apartment. He parked the car but didn't turn off the engine. He leaned over and grabbed Rachel's hand. "Wait here," he said as he turned off the engine and exited the vehicle. He walked around to Rachel's side of the car and opened the door. "Work is over for now," he said with a smile.

Rachel laughed and grabbed his hand as she exited the vehicle, pulling her purse and tote bag behind her. "No more partners, huh?"

"Not tonight," he said. Rachel thought it was nice to have someone treat her with such respect. Todd took the tote to lighten her load, and the two walked down the hall at a medium pace. Rachel dug her keys out of her purse. Todd gently reached over and put his hands on her keys. "May I?" he asked. "Just in case."

"Sure, good idea," Rachel answered, hoping they were being a little over-paranoid. She took a deep breath as Todd opened the door. He entered first as Rachel scanned the apartment from the doorway. Nothing looked out of place this time. Todd dropped the bag on Rachel's floor as looked in each of the rooms with his weapon drawn, and after being satisfied that they were in the clear, lowered his gun and motioned for Rachel to enter. She closed the door behind her, and Todd moved to lock it behind her. "Do I have time for a quick shower?" Rachel asked.

Todd looked at the clock on Rachel's oven. 5:43 pm. "Um, yeah, I think so," he answered as he moved toward the couch to sit.

Rachel smiled, disappeared into her bedroom with her tote and closed the door. She climbed in the shower and let the hot water wash away the stress of the past

118

day. She finished up quickly and went to her closet. She pulled out fresh clothes for a few days. She wasn't sure what her plan was, exactly, and she tended to overpack, just in case. She thought about the conversation Todd had with her this morning. What did he mean by that, she wondered. Maybe that was his way of sending her back home? Rachel kept playing the conversation in her head. Playing with fire because he liked the rush, she thought to herself. She swapped out some of the clothes she had put in the bag for ones she considered less flattering and decided not to try to impress Todd for dinner. Less fire, she thought. She slid on jeans and a pull over tunic. She brushed and dried her hair and decided to forego the extra makeup. Whatever was still on from the shower would be ok for tonight, she told herself. After she was ready, Rachel left the bedroom, the tote still on her bed. She didn't want to be presumptuous about staying with Todd again, especially after that weird speech he gave her this morning. "Ready?" she asked.

Todd stood up and smiled. He held out his hand, and she reached for his. "No, where is your bag?" he laughed.

"Oh," Rachel said cheerfully as she dropped his hand and tried to think of something to say. Nothing came to mind. She must have looked like a bimbo to him. Finally, she said, "I wasn't sure what my plans were."

Todd smiled and said, "Well, you aren't staying here alone."

Again, with the vague answers. "I can call Sara. I'm sure she wouldn't mind," Rachel said, fishing.

"No, don't," Todd said.

Rachel turned and walked toward her bedroom, happy that Todd wasn't ditching her. She grabbed the tote and handed it to him. Rachel was almost giddy with excitement of a mystery dinner and staying with Todd again. She knew she needed to back off, but she enjoyed being with him so much. Todd said, "So, I have to warn you. My mom is going to try to show you every picture of when I was a kid."

"What?" Rachel asked, confused by the reference.

"My mom is a matchmaker, and she has this sick, twisted sense of reality in which showing a woman embarrassing baby pictures magically creates an unbreakable bond."

Rachel laughed at the thought. "She might be onto something!" Rachel teased. She must live in Collierville. And they were going to her house for dinner. Rachel was ashamed she didn't put it together earlier.

Todd smiled, "Well, in that case, you can look at them twice!" Rachel smiled but was immediately uncomfortable with where Todd wanted this to go, and he sensed it. "No, seriously, though, my mother lives for this kind of stuff. She's going to tell you all kinds of crazy stories, so don't you believe them."

"She can't be that bad, Todd," Rachel said.

"Nah, she means well," Todd said. "And don't be worried about imposing. She is lonely in that house by herself and welcomes the company, trust me."

Imposing? Rachel was staying with Todd's mother? Rachel tried not to let the shock and disappointment show on her face, but her body language screamed her level of discomfort. "Look, Rachel," Todd started.

"No, it's fine. It makes sense. I just shouldn't impose like this. I need to make my own arrangements and stop putting you and your family out," Rachel said.

"You are not 'putting me out', Rachel" Todd argued. "I want to do this. My mom – believe me – my mom really wants to do this," Todd said as he rolled his eyes and smiled.

Rachel wasn't really sure how to react. She thought Jimma was funny and probably did welcome the company. And staying at Todd's probably wasn't the best call on date number two, even if there were extenuating circumstances. "But –" was all she could muster to come out.

Todd reached for her hand and pulled her into a hug. "Rachel, we are going to work the case. Sometimes it takes more than a day to solve a mystery, and I want you to feel safe while we do this. Ok?" Rachel liked the feel of his muscles wrapped around her. She closed her eyes and enjoyed the feel of protection in his arms. She wanted him to kiss her. Instead he backed out of the hug and dropped his hands to meet hers. "You good?" he asked.

Rachel nodded and said, "Yeah, ok, but I need to take my car."

Todd wasn't thrilled with the thought of Rachel being out of his sight, but he knew he needed to give her some space, especially after springing on her that she'd be staying with his mom. "Ok, that's fine. You can just follow me, but the address is 2341 Maple Mill Road. It's in Maple Grove subdivision just off Poplar past the Kroger on the right," Todd said.

"I think I know where that is. I can find it anyway," Rachel said.

Chapter 22

Todd was relieved that Rachel's car was close behind his all the way to Collierville. They pulled into the drive within seconds of one another, and got out. Rachel liked how the sun in the evening lit up the front of the house. It was a red brick, two-story house with a three-car garage and huge windows. Rachel noticed that the front lawn was perfectly maintained. As they approached the house, Jimma flung the door open and greeted them on the porch. "Oh, great. Y'all are here. I was just about to put an APB out on you," Jimma said as she reached for Rachel's hands and kissed her cheek. "So glad to have you, honey!"

"Thank you, Jimma. I really appreciate you letting me come," Rachel said.

"Yeah, Ma, thanks for this," Todd said as he entered the house.

"Oh, don't be silly. I'm thrilled to help out and to get to know my baby's sweetheart!" Jimma said as Rachel blushed. "Come in, come in, doll. I'll grab the rolls out of the oven so we can eat."

Rachel entered the house slowly and looked around. The foyer was two stories with a wooden floor and huge window overlooking the front yard. There was a wrap-around staircase with a balcony to her right and a dining room to her left with a decorative ceiling. "I'm going to put this in the guest room, Ma," Todd called out as he disappeared down the hall. The house was newer than Rachel had anticipated and seemed very well decorated for a cop's widow, Rachel thought.

"Here, sit, sit, sit. You must have had a busy day," Jimma said, motioning to a dining room chair as she brought the rolls in and moved dishes around to put them in the middle of the table. "I have some coke-colas in the fridge if you'd rather have them. I just put the tea on the table." Jimma offered.

"Oh, thank you. Is it sweet?" Rachel asked.

"Is there any other kind?" Jimma asked rhetorically and laughed. Rachel shared the view.

"This is perfect, Jimma. Thank you," Rachel said as she sipped the tea. "It smells wonderful."

Todd entered the room and plopped in the chair across from Rachel. "Ain't nothing like momma's fried chicken and green beans!" Todd said as he handed Rachel the dish of chicken to take and pass. The three dug into the meal.

Rachel laughed to herself. She loved fried chicken, but she had no idea how to make it. The potatoes, she could handle. And maybe the deviled eggs. Perhaps

Jimma would teach her one day. And then she caught herself thinking about a future with Todd and nearly choked on the chicken.

"You ok, sweetie?" Jimma asked, handing her another napkin. "Todd, hand me that napkin over there at your brother's place."

"No, I'm fine," Rachel said, embarrassed.

"So, any leads on your break-in?" Jimma asked as she offered everyone more tea.

"Some, Ma. Do you remember anything else about that couple we talked about this morning?"

"Esther and J.P.? Not really." Jimma said as she took a bite of potatoes and looked at the wall behind Todd. "Now how in all that is good and mighty in this world did you get there?" she said, talking to a bug on the wall. Jimma stood up and walked to the wall. She grabbed the bug in her napkin and ran to the kitchen to throw it away. "I just had the bug man out here last week. You'd think I was offering free rent or something," she said from the kitchen. "She had a gambling problem," Jimma said as she reentered the room.

"Who?" Todd asked.

"Esther Adams. You know how the ladies gossip. I remember Helen saying she had a gambling problem," Jimma said. "Do you need me to ask around about her at the club? I can be very discreet," Jimma said in a whisper.

"No, Ma. Thanks, though," Todd answered with a smile.

"Well, ok then," Jimma said, whining about not being asked to help.

"Ma -" Todd grabbed her hand.

Jimma jerked her hand away from Todd, "No, that's ok. I understand. You kiddos have your own way of doing thing these days. You don't need an old lady like me getting in your way."

Rachel sensed the tension from the guilt and decided to intervene. "Jimma, how long have you had this house? It's lovely."

"Just a couple of years. I bought it after my Joe passed, bless his soul. I thought it might be too big for me, but the boys keep me company from time to time." Jimma said, smiling at Todd. "I always told your dad I wanted to move away from the city, but he thought he couldn't while he was working downtown. He would probably roll over in his grave if he knew how much I got for that old house you and your brother grew up in."

"Oh, Ma, he wanted you to be happy," Todd reminded Jimma.

"That he did," Jimma agreed, giving Todd's hand a squeeze and pushing back tears. She looked over at Jimma, "Todd is so much like his father." Todd braced himself for what was coming next. "When he was a boy, he brought home every hurt animal he could find. He talked his dad into helping him set up a pet adoption in our neighborhood, once. Do you remember, Todd?"

"I remember you wanted to send the animals to the pound!" Todd argued.

Jimma and Todd laughed. Rachel smiled. "How many were there?" Rachel asked.

Todd looked down at his empty plate. Jimma looked at him and busted out laughing, "Fourteen cats, two rabbits, and three dogs."

"Fourteen cats? I gotta go with your mom on that one, Todd," Rachel said as she laughed. She thought about what that said about Todd as a person. His mother had mentioned strays that morning and thought she was a troubled woman Todd felt sorry for and took in. He must have the gift of mercy, she thought. Rachel liked that thought and wondered how many people he must have helped while being a cop.

Rachel listened to more stories about Todd as a child, as Jimma bragged about Todd's need to do things the right way, to always be the pleasing child, and to volunteer at church. The version of Todd that she was hearing was far from the flirtatious tough guy that she had agreed to have dinner with a few days ago. She liked the witty banter they enjoyed, but it was this version of Todd she really liked.

Rachel helped Jimma clear the table, but Jimma insisted that she not help with the kitchen. "You kids go on and sit in the den. Leave me to my work. I'll be a long in a jiffy," she said.

Rachel and Todd obeyed and retreated to the living room. Rachel noticed the gas logs and fireplace full of family photos. She wandered over to the mantle and looked at the pictures. Todd walked up behind her and pointed over her shoulder to one to her left. "That's me and my dad on a mission trip in Honduras." He smiled and put his arm around her waist. Rachel noticed his eyes lit up when he spoke about his father, and it made her smile. "And that one there, is of us in Alaska building houses for the natives. My dad loved mission trips. I couldn't decide if it was because he loved Jesus so much or he just loved being outdoors. The man was always dragging us camping or on a mission trip. I think I spent my entire childhood in a tent."

"Sounds like a character. You must have loved him a lot, huh?" Rachel asked.

"More than you know. What about your dad?" Todd asked.

Rachel swallowed hard. "Oh, um, I don't know."

Todd looked at her strangely, "You don't know? Well what is he like?"

Rachel's smile faded, "I don't know. He, um, he left when I was six." Rachel pulled away from Todd.

Todd's heart nearly broke as he reached for her hand. "Oh, I'm sorry, Rachel. I didn't know."

128

Rachel put her hand to her forehead and started to speak when she was interrupted by Jimma from the kitchen, "Who wants peach cobbler?"

Rachel darted toward the kitchen. "Oh, I do. Let me help you, Jimma," she said, happy for the distraction. Todd slowly walked that way and got his plate. The three sat on the couch and ate the cobbler as Jimma regaled them of stories about Todd as a boy. Rachel laughed at the stories and enjoyed peeling the layers of Todd's personality.

Jimma had been listening to their conversation before the cobbler and knew there was much for Todd and Rachel to discuss that was none of her business. She had planned an entire evening of sharing about Todd's childhood but recognized that her son had already bonded with this beautiful woman and needed time to build on it without her interruption. "Well, dear, let me show you the bedroom and where everything is," Jimma started. Rachel followed her and got the nickel tour. "Now I'm right down the hall if you need me, sweetie. I'm going to take a bath while you and Todd chat a little longer."

Jimma was a character and a typical Southern momma, but Rachel could tell she had nothing but good intentions where her boy was concerned. She came across as brash and demanding, but in the end, Rachel could see she was more than willing to give him space when he needed it. Rachel came back to the den to find Todd sitting on the couch waiting for her. She sat down next to him and grabbed his hand. Todd smiled at her.

129

"Think you'll survive here with my mom tonight?" he asked.

"Oh, I think we'll do just fine," Rachel answered. "Listen, I have some work I have to do tomorrow. And don't you have to go to the precinct?"

"Oh yeah. Captain will have my head on a platter if I don't work my shift tomorrow. So, we'll have to put our investigation on hold for a day or so, ok?" Todd asked.

"It's kind of frustrating. We were gone all day, and we aren't much closer than we were this morning. Doesn't that bother you?" Rachel answered.

"I guess you get used to it after a while. We probably can bet that J.P. Jones took that plea deal because he was mixed up in something illegal and had someone to protect," Todd offered.

"Not that I have a clue what that has to do with our box or that invitation," Rachel said.

"We'll figure it out. Sometimes it just takes a while."

"Oh, speaking of the box, where is it?"

"I put it in a precinct locker," Todd said. "Remember, Brock? I asked him to do that."

Rachel thought for a minute. "Oh, is that the guy behind the desk?"

"Yeah, he said he'd put it in a locker for me," Todd replied.

"Oh, I remember now. Marcus was flirting with me, so I had forgotten," Rachel said with a smile.

"Oh, Marcus you remember flirting with, but not the parole officer," Todd teased back.

"I didn't say I was flirting with Marcus. I said Marcus was flirting with me."

"Oh, another technicality. That's apparently your specialty."

"You know what else is my specialty?" Rachel said, wanting to banter, but not really thinking before she spoke.

"What?" Todd asked.

Rachel paused and then busted out laughing. "I got nothing. I set it up, and I got nothing."

Todd laughed and watched her face as she giggled. Suddenly, he stopped laughing and put his right hand on her left cheek. He looked her in the eyes and said, "Rachel Parks, you are amazing. You know that?"

Rachel was visibly rattled. She liked the compliment but wished Todd wasn't a cop. She reached up slowly and grabbed his hand with both of hers. She gripped his hand and slowly pushed it down to his leg. She needed to set the record straight before someone got hurt. She was going to have to tell him that they couldn't date. "Todd —"

Todd could feel the brush off coming and wanted to avoid it. He was holding out hope that he could change her mind about cops. "You know, it's late. I need to go," Todd said quickly as he stood up.

"No, wait —" Rachel protested. "I want to talk to you about something."

"I'll catch up with you tomorrow, ok?" Todd leaned down and kissed her on the head as he headed for the hallway.

Rachel smiled and caved, "Ok. Thanks for everything, Todd."

"See you tomorrow," he said as he headed or the door.

Rachel sank in the couch. She was in way over her head with Todd. She liked him, and that was the problem. She knew better than to get involved with a cop. How had things progressed so quickly? She wanted to ring Sara's neck for getting her involved. She had only planned to have one date with the guy and now she was staying at his mother's house? This was insane. She needed to put a stop to it. But he was so great...

Chapter 23

Rachel got lost in her thoughts, with more of them daydreaming about being with Todd than ending it, when Jimma appeared. "Well, did my boy already leave?" she asked.

Rachel was a little startled. "Yes, ma'am."

Jimma sighed, "Well, good!" Jimma walked toward Rachel on the couch and sat down next to her, patting her leg. "Now we can just have some girl time!" Rachel smiled. "So, tell me all about your business."

Rachel told Jimma about her dream to be in advertising and what the plan was for her full-service agency. She got a little carried away detailing the office plans, but Jimma seemed to eat it up. The more Rachel spoke, the more Jimma was engaged. She interrupted Rachel with questions from time to time and let out "oohs" and "ahhs" at all the right places. She was either really interested or a very good pretender. Rachel wasn't sure which, and didn't seem to care.

"I like a woman who has a vision," Jimma said. "you know, the Proverbs 31 woman had her own business."

Rachel thought the comment was odd. "Well, I'm not sure that I'll ever measure up to that woman. She seemed to not have any flaws."

"Nonsense," Jimma said. "There's something special about you, Rachel. I see it, and my boy sees it." Rachel was instantly uncomfortable, and Jimma recognized it. "Rachel, honey, the Proverbs 31 woman was described through the eyes of her man. She was perfect and blameless in his eyes because he loved her. It's a picture of how God sees us once we've accepted Jesus. Perfect and blameless."

Rachel thought about that for a minute. She had never equated the two before. She had always thought about how inferior she was to this legendary woman in the Bible and how no one could ever live up to her. "Is that how Joe saw you?" Rachel asked.

Jimma was taken back by the question. "Well, you know, I don't know. I do know he loved me sacrificially, and that's all any woman can really ask."

Rachel was a little confused by her response. How could she not know how her husband felt about her? Rachel thought that must be the difference between their generations. "Jimma, can I ask you something?"

"Of course, dear," Jimma answered.

"What was it like? To be married to a cop?"

Jimma smiled, "Oh honey," she said as she leaned in to give Rachel a hug. In that moment Jimma knew that

Rachel feared a relationship with her son based on what he did for a living. "Joe was a cop, but that's just what he did. It wasn't who he was."

Rachel pushed back from the hug. "But it was, wasn't it? I mean, he went there every day, putting his life on the line for someone else while you sat at home wondering if he'd come back to you, right? And then, he eventually didn't come home one day, right?" Rachel instantly wished she hadn't blurted that out. It was incredibly insensitive of her. Rachel covered her mouth, and before Jimma could speak, she said, "Oh, I'm sorry, Jimma. I didn't mean —"

"Oh sweetie, it's ok," Jimma said with a smile, stroking her arm. "I worried more about Joe on his mission trips than I did him not coming home from work. He was a good cop, and a good husband. I learned a long time ago that I was not in control of the things in this world. God has given that reign to Satan and his demons, and no amount of worry on my part is going to change that."

Rachel felt a tear come down her face. "You seem to have it all together."

Jimma laughed. "Oh, honey, not even close. I've had my share of demons that I've let stir up strife in my life and made plenty of my own mistakes." Jimma slapped the couch as she got up. "Well, it's about my bedtime. You need anything else before I turn in?"

"No, thank you, Jimma. I'm fine."

"Well, all righty then," Jimma said as she started toward the hall. She turned one last time and smiled at Rachel. "You know, Rachel," she said, "Todd is a cop, but it isn't who he is either."

Rachel smiled and watched Jimma leave the room. She let Jimma's words sink in a little before grabbing her phone. She flipped to the daily devotion and scanned through it. She tried to focus on the words, but all that was going on was distracting to her. She breathed deeply and read aloud, hoping that would help her concentration. Finally, she managed to at least digest the devotion and say a mediocre prayer. She included thanking God for His provision with Todd and asked for his protection moving forward. She asked forgiveness for her initial thoughts about Todd and thanked God for giving Todd a sense of duty in protecting their relationship. She ended the prayer and decided to call Sara. It was about time to get her up to speed. Rachel dialed the number and started talking to Sara, who of course, wanted to start with her date with Todd from last night. It seemed so long ago to Rachel that she nearly forgot that it had only been 24 hours. Rachel was able to move the conversation away from the date once she mentioned that Todd took her to his spirit-filled church. Sara thought that was weird and decided she didn't like Todd for Rachel anymore. Rachel explained the break-in and told Sara about the angel box. Sara was terrified.

"Then just give them the box, Rachel," Sara screamed into the phone.

"Who? Give who the box, Sara?"

"I don't know. Whoever is after it," Sara said, exacerbated.

"Well, if I knew that, I might. Aren't you the least bit curious why someone wants the box?"

"No, not really. It's a box," Sara said.

"UUUGGGH!" Rachel growled at the phone. "Ok, listen, I'm not going to the office tomorrow. Can you take another set of Sam's concepts to his building?"

"What time?"

"9."

"No, I have a meeting with Medtec at 8:30. Jason got me in. We've been trying to see them for months."

"Ok, fine. I can take care of it. I'll just have to leave here early," Rachel said, almost under her breath.

"Early? You live like 5 minutes from the office."

Rachel instantly regretted the slip. "Yeah, I'm in Collierville —"

"Collierville? What's in Collierville?"

"Just staying with a friend," Rachel said, hoping to sneak it by Sara.

"A friend? You have a friend in Collierville?"

"Ok, fine, I'm staying with Todd's mom. Just until —"

Sara busted out laughing. "What? You are staying with his mom? Are you insane?"

"At this point, yes, I think I might be. It's just for a day or two, until we figure out who wants the box."

"We? You are working on this with Todd, aren't you? Rachel, I know I was all gung ho for you to go out with him, but the man took you to a holy roller church with those people who speak in tongues on date number two, and now you are staying with his mom. Hello? Surely, you can see this is weird. You've gotten sucked into to some creepy nightmare."

Rachel knew her friend meant well, but she didn't have a clue what was going on. It wasn't a creepy nightmare, and that was the problem. Still, she knew it was best not to argue with Sara. "I know, I know. Look, I'll see you tomorrow, ok?"

"Ok, but if they hack you to pieces and leave you in the closet for dead, don't expect me to run in and save you," Sara said jokingly.

"Good night, Sara."

"Night."

Chapter 24

Rachel dropped her phone when the alarm went off, which meant she had to get out of bed. She stretched and found her way to the chair where her bag was. She pulled out clothes and hopped into the shower adjacent to her room. She tried to be quiet so as to not wake Jimma. Rachel wasn't sure she could take Jimma's bubbly personality that early. After getting dressed, Rachel made her way to the kitchen and saw a note on the fridge.

"OJ inside. Plate in the microwave. -J"

Rachel smiled and opened the microwave to find a plate of food Jimma had prepared, complete with biscuits and gravy. Rachel happily warmed up the food and enjoyed every bite. She finished getting dressed and headed out with her bag packed.

The road to Sam's office wasn't that far from where she was, but she had to trek into town to get the boards from the old office. She turned on the radio and sang along. It was nearly a two-hour round-trip drive from Collierville to the office and back out to Arlington. She had to use the GPS on her phone to tell her how to get to Sam's office. It was further out than she thought.

Once she arrived, Rachel gathered the boards and went in to see Sam. She was only supposed to drop the boards off, but Sam wanted to talk to her. She had spent an hour with him after it was all said and done. Rachel wondered if Sara was available. She tapped the right buttons on her phone to speed dial Sara and stood in the lobby to talk to her. Rachel knew her car would be hot by now.

Sara answered the phone, "You're not going to believe this!"

"What?" Rachel asked.

"I got us an RFP!" Sara screamed.

"Medtec? They want a proposal?" Rachel asked, almost in shock.

"Yeah. Awesome, right? And get this. It's not just for one project, Rachel. It's to be a preferred vendor!" Sara shouted.

"No way! That's fantastic. How did you pull that off?" Rachel asked.

"They were ripe for the pickin' for sure. One of their agencies blew it big time last month," Sara said.

"Wonder which one."

"You know which one. It had to be Green Velvet," Sara offered.

"Of course. Well, good for us, right?"

"Right. Whoo-hoo!" Sara shouted.

"I have good news for you, too, Sara."

"Oh yeah, what's that?" Sara asked.

"The information architecture for Sam's site is approved as is. He just needed the extra set of concept boards to show at a meeting."

"Want to celebrate over lunch?" Sara asked.

"Sure, but where are you?"

"I'm in Bartlett. How about you?" Sara asked.

"In Arlington. We could meet at the mall in Cordova," Rachel offered.

"Ok, but none of that food court mess. Let's do El Ranchero outside the mall," Sara said.

Rachel laughed to herself. Sara was so predictable. "Ok, meet you there in a few."

Chapter 25

The cheese dip came out first. Rachel dug in, dipping them in salsa, guacamole and salsa again, while Sara picked at chips on the table and ate them plain.

Sara raised her tea glass up and said, "To us!"

Rachel smiled and reciprocated. "To our company, indeed!"

The two clinked the glasses together gently and drank a sip of tea. "Now for the good stuff. What's going on with the hot cop and his psycho family fantasy?"

"It's not a fantasy, and he's not psycho!" Rachel insisted.

"You gotta admit, though, it's a little weird. Right?" Sara said.

Rachel dipped another chip and piled it into her mouth. She chewed for a moment and then answered. "Sara, someone was in my apartment. You think it's crazy that he is trying to protect me?"

"I think it's crazy that he sent you to stay with his mom! I mean, come on, who does that? Why didn't you come to my place if you were scared?" Sara asked.

Rachel thought about that for a minute and started to answer when suddenly a server appeared with their food. "Taco with beans and rice?" she asked.

Sara raised her hand, and the woman sat the plate down in front of Sara. She reached for the other plates and put them in front of Rachel. "Do you need anything else?" she asked.

Rachel scanned the plate to see her order was fulfilled correctly, complete with the extra chili peppers. "I think we are all set," Rachel answered.

"Sara, you have a lot on your plate with Jason. I didn't want to intrude," Rachel said.

"So, you thought you'd stay at some guy's mom's house. I'm sure you weren't intruding at all there," Sara said sarcastically.

"Sara, he just wanted to protect me. That's all."

"Yeah, and if something happens to you, he can just channel the spirits from his church and heal you," Sara said, crunching her taco.

"That's not fair, Sara," Rachel said.

Sara finished chewing her bite and responded, "Maybe not." She paused and then asked, "So what's the deal?"

"I don't know," Rachel said as she fiddled with her fork.

"You still like him?" Sara asked, knowing the answer was yes.

"He's different."

"Are you talking about the weird church date? Because I agree with you that is different," Sara said.

Rachel put her fork down and leaned forward across the table. "Sara, do you know why I never date lawyers and doctors and cops?"

Sara recounted the words, rolling her eyes with each syllable, "Because your momma always said be careful who you date, blah, blah, blah. I've heard it a million times from you."

"No, I mean, yes, but there's more to it than that. My dad left when I was six. He was a doctor. He was always on call, and my mom said he was never around when it mattered anyway. And when he was, mom said he was always talking about work. He ran off with his nurse, and he never looked back."

Sara stopped eating and grabbed Rachel's hand and squeezed. Rachel felt tears welling up in her eyes. "She said that all doctors and lawyers and cops were the same way. Married to their work and prone to cheat."

"Rachel, eliminating the guys you date by their profession won't weed out the bad seeds," Sara said.

Rachel wiped her right eye. "Yeah, I know, but it's a good starting point, right?"

Sara laughed. "No, it's not."

Rachel chuckled.

"You know, it's ok to be cautious," Sara offered.

"Yeah?"

"Yeah."

Rachel's smile grew to fill her whole face. "So, when is he going to kiss me?"

Sara's mouth dropped open. "You still haven't kissed him?"

"Well, no, he hasn't kissed me. I didn't want to initiate it," Rachel said.

Sara laughed so loud she covered her mouth. "What? Rachel Parks, Ms. I'm going to do it my way right now with or without you, Rachel Parks, didn't want to initiate something? Since when have you been shy?"

"Reserved. And only when it comes to guys. I'm just not comfortable making the first move."

"You could have fooled me with all that flirty conversation you guys do with one another."

"That's different. And, I didn't expect it to go anywhere," Rachel said.

Sara sat up in her seat. "And this is? Going somewhere?"

Before Rachel could answer, Sara's phone rang. She answered it after seeing that it was Jason. "Hey, babe. What's up?" Sara paused for an answer. "Yeah, ok, I'm on my way," she said and hung up. "Ok, I gotta go. Jason's car won't start. He's got to go in early for some training thing. But we are not done with this conversation!" Sara grabbed her bag and left the restaurant.

Rachel was relieved not to have to answer the question. The truth was that she didn't know where it was going, and it had already gone further than she thought it should. She needed to wrap up this whole box mystery sooner rather than later. She wondered how far Braden was. There was still the brother that she wanted to talk to about the invitation. She googled Braden and saw that it was less than 20 miles from her. She thought she might as well head that direction and see what she could find out. Besides, Todd was busy today anyway, she thought.

Chapter 26

Rodney finished his Big Gulp from the 7 Eleven with a loud slurp and finished chewing his burrito just as his phone rang again. He had been watching the house on Oak Trail for any sign of Rachel since last night. Rodney looked down to see Shane's number on the caller ID. "What is it?" he barked at the phone.

"Derrick picked up the girl's car."

"Then why are we talking? Go get the red dove?" Rodney asked.

"It's not that simple. She's in public," Shane said.

"Where?"

"At the mall," Shane answered.

Rodney let out a sign and ran his fingers through his hair. "Do I have to think of everything? Tail her until she's alone and then get it done. If we don't find that red dove soon, we are all going to be at the bottom of the Mississippi."

"Where do you want me to take her when we grab her?"

Rodney took the phone and banged it on the steering wheel three times. "What part of 'quietly' don't you understand? Don't grab her. Just search her and the car for the package. Find a way to do that without kidnapping her."

"How do you suggest we do that?" the voice said.

"Be creative," Rodney said as he angrily punched the phone off and threw it across the passenger seat. He banged his head on the steering wheel several times and wondered if they were going to find it in time to satisfy his boss. The phone rang again. Rodney debated answering it. He picked it up and after seeing the caller ID, he decided he had to answer it.

"Yeah, Boss," he said.

"Report," the gruff voice instructed.

"We tracked the girl's car down. My guys won't let her slip away. Once she's isolated, we'll search for the package. We got this, Boss," Rodney said, trying to convince himself more than his boss.

Chapter 27

Braden was an extremely small town. Rachel passed the fire department and wondered if there was a city hall where she could find Martin Adam's property records. She spotted the only restaurant in town, Braden Station, and decided to pull in and see what she could find out. She entered the restaurant and was greeted from across the room by a waitress dressed in jeans and tennis shoes with her brown hair pulled in a ponytail. "Sit wherever you like, and I'll be right with you," she said.

Rachel said, "Oh, I was just wondering if you knew Martin Adams."

"Marty?" the waitress said. "Everybody knows Marty."

"Do you happen to know where I can find him?"

"He's probably at the fire station. Usually goes there after tending to the animals."

"Thanks," Rachel said as she turned to exit the restaurant.

"No problem," the waitress said as she continued setting tables.

Rachel drove back to the fire station and parked outside the building. As she exited the vehicle, she spotted two men smoking cigarettes outside the door. They were dressed in dirty jeans and button-down shirts. One man had a beard, but the other one was clean shaven. Neither were particularly attractive. Both turned her way, and the one with a beard yelled, "You need some help, little lady?"

The other one laughed as he said, "Yeah, we are trained in mouth-to-mouth." He immediately took a gut punch from his friend.

Rachel rolled her eyes, as the men approached her. "How can we help you?" the clean-shaven man asked.

"I'm looking for Marty Adams."

"Well, you found him," the bearded man said. "What can I do for you?"

"It's about your mother's house. I have a couple of questions," Rachel said.

"You'd have to talk to the lawyer about all that. He handles all the estate stuff," Marty said.

"Oh, no, I'm not here for money or anything. I just wanted to ask you a couple of questions about your mother. Please, Mr. Adams," Rachel said.

Marty hesitated and then motioned for her to come into the fire station. "I don't know what you need, but my momma and I weren't exactly on the best of terms."

"I'm sorry to hear that. What about your sister?"

"Esther? That lying witch? She's the reason my mom and I were not close anymore. She always had some scheme up her sleeve - just couldn't just be happy with the talent she was given; she always had to have more."

Rachel was intrigued by this family feud and thought it might play into the box. "What do you mean by talent?"

"Esther was a painter. She was good, too. She could paint anything – Monet, Rembrandt, Dali, you name it."

"Sounds like she was very talented."

"She was. I tried to get her to open her own studio, but she didn't like doing her own work. She liked copying other people's art. And, she was more interested in gambling than she was painting. But Momma thought she hung the moon and that she could do no wrong."

Rachel asked, "She was about to get married, wasn't she?"

"Oh yeah, to some scumbag art thief. But he killed her first, the sorry–"

"Art thief? J.P. was an art thief?"

"Well, art, coins, stamps – something like that. He and Esther cooked up some big job and convinced my mother it was the answer to all her money troubles, as usual. Mother only had money problems because of Esther, but you couldn't convince her of that. Anyway, I guess it went sideways, and that's why he killed Esther."

Money troubles, Rachel thought. "Do you know what it was they were working on?"

"Lady, if I did, I would have already told the cops. I didn't like my sister much, but what J.P. did ain't right." Rachel thought about what they could have been doing for a minute. "Who did you say you were with again?" Marty asked.

Rachel realized it was time to go. "Oh, I, um, I, thank you for your time," Rachel said as she walked quickly toward the door and out to her car.

Rachel sped away from the firehouse quickly wondering if she had stepped into trouble. She drove down the road thinking about what Marty had told her. Todd said the box wasn't that valuable. Was he wrong? She reached into her purse to call him, and remembered she didn't have his phone number. She had texted from Sara's phone and never cleared that up with him. She would have to call Sara to get it and then explain it to Todd. Not something she was interested in doing. Rachel decided just to drive to the precinct and talk to him in person. She tossed the phone in the passenger seat as she sped down the road. It was a narrow road without much traffic. Rachel turned up the radio and sang along. She wanted to honk her horn at a red F150 pickup that passed her in a no passing zone as if she were standing still, but she refrained.

Suddenly, Rachel entered a curve to find that red F150 pickup sitting still in her lane. She didn't have much road to work with before slamming into it. There was water to her right, so she reacted by stomping on the breaks and swerving to the left. Her car careened off the road into the ditch. The tires slid on the muddy embankment, and the front nose of the Mustang hit a mud hill and stopped instantly. Since it was an older car, there were no airbags. Although she hadn't been going that fast at the time of impact, it was enough to throw her forward. Rachel smacked her head hard on the steering wheel at the point of impact.

She was dazed from the head trauma and felt her seat belt locked onto her body. She reached up to her forehead to check for blood and felt woozy. She reached to open the door, but it was being held closed by the embankment. Just then, two men came up from behind her car and started talking. Rachel started to ask for help, but her voice was weak, "He —" was all she could get out. Instead of helping, the men grabbed her purse out of the passenger side. The fuzziness in her head prevented her from hearing much of their conversation, but she could tell they were looking through her purse for something. She heard one of the men say, "red dove" before everything went black.

Chapter 28

"Welcome back," the nurse said standing over Rachel's body, checking her fluids as Rachel opened her eyes. "You've been out for a while. I'll get the doctor. Do you know your name, honey?"

Rachel started to speak, but her mouth was dry. "Rachel."

"Good, ok, honey. My name is Tracy, and I'm going to be taking care of you tonight. Let me grab the doctor, ok?"

The nurse left the room and disappeared down the hallway. Rachel checked out her surroundings. She was clearly in a hospital bed with an IV and a hospital gown. She wondered how the nurses managed to change her clothes. She looked to her right and saw there was a phone and started to reach for it. The wires connecting her to the IV and heart monitor were in the way. As she reached to pull them back, the doctor entered the room.

"Good evening. The nurse tells me your name is Rachel. Is that right?" The young doctor seemed overly excited to be in Rachel's room. He looked to be about 25.

Rachel could only make out big details, like he had brown hair and a goatee, as her vision was still blurry.

"Yes," Rachel answered in a whisper.

"Well, Rachel, you have quite a nasty bump on your head. Do you remember how you got that?"

"An accident," Rachel said, again in a whisper.

"Ok, good," the doctor said as he flashed a light in her eyes and pulled at her eyelids. "Rachel, I'm going to send you down for an MRI, just to make sure we don't have any swelling on the brain, ok." Rachel could tell it was more of a directive, not a question.

"I need to call --" Rachel started.

"After the MRI, we'll get all that settled. For now, I need to make sure we don't have any serious bleeding to contend with. Ok? Ok. I'll see you after the scan." The doctor turned toward the nurse and said, "Call imaging and let them know we have an emergency scan," as he handed the nurse the chart and exited the room.

The nurse approached Rachel and started pulling wires and arranging them on the bed. "I need to call my friend," she said to the nurse, her head pounding.

"I know, honey, we'll call him as soon as we get back, ok? The doctor wants this done immediately. Are you wearing anything metal?"

Rachel wanted to be smart and say that she should know since she dressed her, but she knew the nurse was just doing her job. "I don't think so," Rachel answered.

The nurse started to push the bed out of the room and said, "Just relax, sweetie. This is a piece of cake."

Rachel worried about what time it was and if Jimma and Todd had noticed she hadn't come back to the house yet.

The nurse wheeled the bed down to imaging, and parked it outside a room labeled "MRI". Rachel wasn't sure how long she sat outside the room before they pulled her in, but she didn't see how this could have ranked as dealing with an emergency scan. It seemed like an hour or more before it was her turn, but her vision cleared, and her headache settled to a dull roar. Finally, the door opened and another nurse pulled Rachel's bed into the room. Rachel followed the instructions and participated in the long scan which she was told would last 45 minutes.

After the scan was over, the nurse rolled her back out into the hallway and said, "I've called for transport. They should be here in a few minutes."

Rachel waited what seemed like another hour before a dark-haired man in scrubs came to push her to her room. She was anxious to let Todd know where she was, but she knew she'd have to call Sara to get through to him. And that definitely wouldn't be pleasant. As they approached the room, Rachel started to tell the nurse that she needed to call her friend. He didn't understand what she was saying. He must not speak English, she thought.

As he pushed her into the room, Tracy reappeared. "How is your pain, Rachel? On a scale of 1-10."

Rachel's head hurt, but she didn't really want to be bothered with these questions. She wanted to call Todd and let him know she was ok. She was ok, wasn't she?

"A 5? A 7? How bad?" Tracy asked.

"Um, about a 5, I guess," Rachel said as Tracy started hooking up wires to her again. "I just need to call my friend."

"Oh yes, we'll do that, ok? Just let me finish this up, and then I'll get you some pain medicine," Tracy said as she worked.

"I really need to let my friend know I'm ok," Rachel said reaching for the phone.

Tracy reached over and grabbed the phone. "Here ya go. I'll run get you some pain meds and be right back."

Rachel frantically tried to dial Sara's number. It rang about 6 times before her voicemail kicked in. Rachel waited for the beep and left a message, "Sara, this is Rachel. I need you to call me. I'm in the hospital," and then Rachel realized she didn't know which hospital or what room. She scanned the room but couldn't make out anything. "Sara, call Todd and let him know, too, ok? I'll find the room number and call you back." Rachel hung up the phone dialed the operator.

"Saint Francis Hospital. How may I direct your call?

"Um, can you tell me what room number I'm calling from, please?"

"2475," was the answer.

"Ok, thank you," Rachel said. She dialed Sara again. Buzzy signal. She slammed the received down and waited a couple of seconds before dialing again. Buzzy signal again. Rachel put the phone to the side and hoped Sara would figure it out. She'd try again in a few minutes.

Tracy returned with a needle and entered it into the IV attached to Rachel's arm. "This should help you sleep, honey. I'll check on you in a bit," she said.

Rachel tried to stay awake, but the medicine was very powerful. She needed to call Sara back and let her know which hospital, but her eyes were heavy, and she drifted off to sleep. She remembered the nurse coming in and out a couple of times, but she was too tired to react.

Chapter 29

Rachel woke up suddenly and realized she had been sweating. She looked around the room and remembered where she was. The sun had not finished rising yet, but it must be close to morning, she thought. She sat up in the bed and started to reach for the phone. She wondered if Todd was concerned about her at all. And why Sara hadn't called back. Rachel caught a glimpse of a figure outside her room and tensed up. She wondered if the men from the accident were after her and what red dove meant. She took a deep breath as the figure pushed the door open.

It was Todd. "Hey, how are you doing?" he asked in a hushed voice, happy to see Rachel sitting up in the bed.

"Aren't you a sight for sore eyes. Did Sara call you?" she asked.

Todd crossed the room to her bed and grabbed her hand. "No, I spent most of the evening searching for you. Once I found you, Nurse Ratchet out there said visiting hours were over and wouldn't let me in. I slept in the lobby until I could sneak past the nurse brigade out there. Don't make too much noise or they'll kick me out, ok?"

Rachel laughed. "What are they going to do, arrest you?"

"Maybe," Todd whispered.

"The doctor wouldn't tell me much. Are you ok?"

"I'm fine," Rachel said and then thought about it again. "Well, I think I am. They did an MRI to make sure there wasn't any swelling, but the doctor never told me what it showed. I guess it was fine."

"What happened, Rachel? The police report says you lost control on Highway 79."

"No, that is not right. Some jerk passed me and then parked in the road in the bend of a curve. I swerved to miss him and hit the ditch. The last thing I remember some rednecks were taking my –" Rachel stopped as she spotted her purse in the floor next to the chair. "purse," she finished.

Todd snapped his head around to see what she was looking at behind him. "Your purse? Isn't this it?" he said as he reached to grab it.

"Yeah, that's weird. I saw them take it. Hmm, maybe they were my good Samaritans and not purse thieves after all."

"I don't think so, Rachel. The police report says an officer found your car, and you were unresponsive."

"How bad is my car?" Rachel asked, afraid of the answer.

"I think we can fix it. I had my buddy Chris take it to his shop on Summer Ave. Just the grill and left headlight are toast. That's the thing about those old cars; they are tanks."

"Yeah, my head can confirm that. Oh, and I found out that – Hey, did you really sleep in the lobby last night?" Rachel asked with a smile on her face.

"Absolutely I did. Rachel, I didn't know what had happened to you. You just disappeared and wouldn't answer my calls. Of course, I came looking for you."

Rachel remembered that he had Sara's phone. "Wait, you called, and I didn't answer?"

"Duh, that's why I went looking for you," Todd said with a smile.

"You don't have my phone number, though. You have Sara's, and she's not answering my calls either."

"What?"

"Yeah, ok. Here it goes," Rachel said as she raised her hands to her face to hide her embarrassment over what she was about to say. "Sara was pushing me to go out with you, so I thought I'd punish her by giving you her phone number. That way, she would have to put up with all the calls."

"Wow," Todd said, stunned. "That's a new one."

"I know. I was going -"

Tracy interrupted, "What are you doing in here? It's not visiting hours! I told you that already, now don't make me call security."

"It's ok, it's ok, he's with me. He's a cop. This is my friend Todd that I was trying to call last night. He was just worried about me."

Tracy was not amused. "Well, that's nice. Now he's seen you, and now he has to go," Tracy said as she started pushing Todd out of the room. "You can come back during visiting hours like everyone else," she said as she pushed him completely out and turned her attention back to Rachel. "I have good news for you. The doctor says you can go home today. You have a ride, honey?"

"I did, but you pushed him out of the room," Rachel said.

"Well, he can come back in an hour when visiting hours start."

An hour? Rachel could not believe that the nurse was being such a stickler for the rules. Rachel started to cry.

"Oh, sweetie, don't cry. It's going to be ok," Tracy said as she handed Rachel a tissue.

"Is it? What if he doesn't come back?" Rachel said loudly. Just then could feel the knots in her stomach. The same ache came over her as the day her dad left.

"In my experience, you are better off without him," Tracy said. "Men are trouble. They love you and leave you for a younger woman. I say make your own way in the world. One where you are in charge of your own life, and that way you can leave them first." Rachel had heard that same message from her mom most of her life. Don't date this type of man or that type of man. They'll leave you for another woman, she had heard. It's why she didn't date cops. Or lawyers. Or doctors. Or anyone. She didn't want to be left. Again.

Rachel didn't want to be hurt again, but all she could think about was how she must have hurt Todd. He had done nothing to betray her trust. In fact, he had gone out of his way to make her feel safe and protected. He had sacrificed his time for her. He had asked his family to sacrifice for her. And she had rewarded him by making him feel unimportant and unwanted. What if he didn't let her make it up to him?

"Tracy, when can I leave?" Rachel asked as she stood up, grabbing the bed for support.

"Well, I need to finish your paperwork up, and the doctor will want to make one last check. I'm getting off shift in thirty minutes, so it will probably have to wait until the next nurse comes in," Tracy said.

"No, I need to leave now," Rachel said with a shot of adrenaline that made her balance return in full force.

"It takes a little time to get the paperwork ready," Tracy said.

"I don't need any paperwork," Rachel said, ripping the wires off her body and yanking the IV out of her arm. The heart monitor started making all kinds of racket as the alarm went off.

Tracy ran to the machine to stop it from beeping. "You can't just leave," she said.

"Why not? You said I'm fine. It's just a matter of paperwork," Rachel said as she grabbed her pants and pulled them up under her gown.

"That's not how it's done," Tracy said as she finished turning the monitor off.

"Well, it's how it's going to be done today," Rachel said pulling her shirt over her head and throwing the gown on the bed.

"Just wait a minute, and I'll get your paperwork together before I leave, ok?" Tracy said.

"Ok, fine," Rachel said as she sat in the chair to put her shoes on. As soon as Tracy left the room, Rachel grabbed her purse and peered out the door. She didn't see anyone in the hallway, so she opened the door carefully and ran down the hallway to what she hoped was the lobby. She came to a "T" in the hall and read the signs to direct herself to the waiting area. She rounded the corner, flushed, to see Todd sitting patiently in a chair. He saw her approach and stood up.

She grabbed his hand and pulled him toward the elevator. "Come on, we have to go," she said.

"What?"

"Just come on before Nurse Ratchet finds us," she said pulling him into the elevator.

"What are you doing, Rachel?" Todd asked.

"Leaving," Rachel said as the doors closed.

"Aren't they supposed to wheel you out in a chair or something?" Todd asked, noticing that Rachel was looking a little pale.

"I don't know. I guess. It's not like I can't walk," Rachel said.

Todd scooped her up in his arms. "Well, then I'll just carry you," he said with a smile as the elevator dinged.

An elderly man was waiting as the doors opened. He saw the two and said, "Oh, I can wait. You two love birds go ahead."

Rachel laughed as Todd carried her out of the elevator. "Excuse us," she said as they brushed passed the man.

"Are you ok?" Todd asked.

"I'm better now. Where is your car?" Rachel asked.

"Just outside emergency," Todd said. As he approached the car, Todd stopped and gently lowered Rachel to her feet. He opened the door, helped her in and closed it behind her. As Todd entered the car he thought for a moment and said, "Wait - did you just escape from the hospital?"

Rachel laughed. "Yeah, I think I did. And you are my accomplice!"

"Why did you do that?"

Rachel blushed, and then she bit her bottom lip. Her smiled faded, and she grabbed Todd by the hand. "I don't know. We had that argument and I -"

"What argument?"

"The phone number –"

"What? Because you wanted to protect yourself from annoying calls after a first date? Rachel, it's fine. I get it."

Rachel smiled, "Yeah?"

"Yeah," Todd said. "We'll talk about it later. Right now, I think we should get out of here."

"Good idea!" Rachel said.

Chapter 30

Rachel woke up slowly from her nap. She looked around the room and realized she must have fallen asleep on the way to Jimma's, and Todd must have carried her into the bedroom so she could rest. Her headache was only a dull ache at this point. She swung her feet over the side of the bed and stood up slowly, using her hands to balance herself against the mattress until her equilibrium recalibrated. She took a few steps toward the door, carefully, until she realized that she was not dizzy anymore. She rounded the corner in the hallway and saw Jimma sitting in the living room on the couch.

Jimma spotted her out of the corner of her eye, yanked off her reading glasses and threw the magazine she was reading down on the couch. She sprang up and ran to Rachel. "Here, dear, let me help you," she said as she reached for Rachel's arm.

"I'm ok, thanks, Jimma," Rachel answered and kept walking to the couch.

"Let me get you something to eat," Jimma said as she disappeared into the kitchen. "I'll just be a minute, sweetie. You get comfortable and let ole Jimma take care of you." She said. Jimma reappeared with a plate of food enough for two and a huge glass of tea. "You must be famished. Is your head hurting, dear? I've got some Tylenol if you need it."

"Thank you, Jimma. I'm ok," she said as she started to eat what was on the plate. About half-way through she said, "Do you know what time it is?" Rachel asked.

"About 3:30 I think."

"3:30!" Rachel said loudly. "Sara must be worried sick. I need to call her."

"I did that this morning. I hope you don't mind, but Todd asked me to call her and explain what was going on."

"Oh," Rachel said, "No, that's good. Did she say why she didn't answer the phone earlier?"

"She said she had gotten a lot of calls from the same number and turned the ringer down," Jimma answered.

Rachel snickered a little, as she thought about how many times Todd must have called her phone in his search. "Jimma," Rachel started, "do you know if there is such a thing as a red dove?"

"A red dove?" Jimma asked. "Doesn't seem like much for peace if it's red, now does it?"

"I guess not," Rachel answered.

"Why do you ask?"

168

"I'm not sure. It's something I thought I heard some men at the accident say."

"Maybe it's some weird code name for a damsel in distress," Jimma smiled.

Rachel smiled. Rachel wondered if she was right. "Jimma, think it would be ok to call Todd?"

"I thought you'd never ask," Jimma said as she handed her phone to Rachel.

Rachel punched up Todd's number from the contacts and called the number showing. Todd answered in one ring. "Hey, Ma, how is she?"

"It's Rachel. I'm fine. Thanks for bringing me to your mom's."

"Well, it sounds like you are feeling better. Hey, you aren't going to try to escape again are you?"

"From here? No way. Jimma is a great hostess!"

"Ok, good, because I'd hate to have to go looking for you again," Todd said through a chuckle. "Oh, hey, Captain is calling me. See you for dinner?"

"Sure."

"Get some rest!"

"I will. Later."

Rachel ended the call on the phone and stared at it for just a couple of seconds and then smiled. Jimma noticed and said, "You do know he had nearly every cop in his precinct looking for you, right?"

Rachel looked down. "Oh, I'm sorry. I didn't mean to worry everyone. I guess I'm becoming more trouble than I'm worth."

Jimma smiled, "Honey, please, that boy would go to the ends of the earth for you."

"Why? He barely knows me."

"Oh, sweetie, he's had his eye on you for a while. Why else do you think he showed up at every event at your church or stopped by your business nearly every day for months on end? He wanted to make sure you were worthy to woo."

Rachel thought about that for a minute and let it sink in. Worthy to woo? Did Jimma actually mean that word or was that Jimma's Southern old-fashioned speak for dating? "And so am I? Worthy to woo?" Rachel asked with a confused look on her face.

"You're sitting on my couch, aren't you?" Jimma said with a smile.

Rachel spent the rest of the afternoon trying to catch up on work items and searching for a random art shows where Esther and J.P. might have planned a theft. There wasn't as much information online as she had hoped, and the search was frustrating. She let her mind wander quite a bit to thoughts of Todd. She liked him, but she wasn't sure about him being a cop. And they never finished talking about that weird church. Things got out of control pretty quickly, and she felt like she went from first date to girlfriend zero to sixty. She wondered why she was so comfortable with Todd and Jimma.

Chapter 31

Todd brought Chinese food from around the corner when he arrived at 8:15. "Sorry I'm late, Ma," Todd said as he sat the bags on the table. "You know how Pastor Brian can get going sometimes."

"It's fine, honey, we ate a late lunch, right Rachel?" Jimma said as she was unpacking the bags onto the table.

"Oh, yeah, it's fine," Rachel said, happy Jimma didn't have to cook. "Which one is Pastor Brian? I thought Mike was the pastor?"

Todd stopped filling up his plate and looked at Rachel, "Oh, Mike is at the Assembly. This is at Hickory Grove." Rachel looked at Todd, confused. "I told you I was a Baptist. I just go to Assembly on Sunday nights because we don't have a service."

"Oh," Rachel said, a little relieved.

"So, Rachel, what were you doing on highway 79 yesterday?" Todd asked.

"Oh, I totally forgot to tell you. I met Esther's brother Marty in Braden."

172

Todd dropped his chop sticks on the table. "What? Why did you go out there without me?"

Rachel took it in stride and didn't stop preparing her next bite. "You were busy, and I thought I might get more information without a cop. I was only like 20 minutes away so I thought I might as well check it out. And it paid off, too. Marty told me that his mother had money troubles, and J.P and Esther had one big job planned that must have gone sideways before he killed her."

"What kind of a job?" Jimma asked

"He claimed he didn't know – said he thought J.P. was an art thief, and Esther was a painter. Sounds like she could forge paintings from his description of her," Rachel answered.

"So maybe the angel box is related to a missing painting?" Todd asked

"Maybe," Rachel said.

"Well, her mother sold a lot of art over the years. Makes sense to me." Jimma said.

"So, we just need to find out what was stolen recently and then maybe we can connect the dots to our box," Todd said.

Rachel frowned. "I've been looking all day and haven't found anything."

"I'm off duty tomorrow. We'll start again in the morning."

Rachel smiled. The three of them finished up dinner and cleared the table. Todd and Rachel moved to the living room and sat on the couch. Jimma excused herself to do some laundry.

"How is my hospital escapee doing? You feeling alright? Not too tired?" Todd asked.

"I fine, really, I am."

"You do know that you will have to deal with that stunt sooner or later, right?"

"Yeah, I'm not sure what came over me. I'll call in the morning. They just want their money. Once I give them my insurance information, tell them I'm not going to sue them, and pay the deductible, they'll be happy. I'm sure I'm not the first person to skip out on them."

Todd laughed. "Probably not."

"Can I ask you something?" Rachel asked.

"You just did," Todd smiled.

"No, I mean for real."

Todd smiled. "Of course."

"What did you do at work today?"

Todd was stunned by the question. "What do you mean?"

"I mean, what did you do at work today?" Rachel knew the question was odd, but she wanted to know what it was like for Todd to be a cop and what her life might be like listening to all the stories about bad guys when he got home.

"Um, I chased bad guys?" Todd said with a confused look on his face.

"I'm being serious. Tell me about the bad guys you chased."

"That's just it. I don't bring the bad guys home with me."

Rachel thought that was strange and wonderful all at the same time. "Really?" she asked.

"Really."

"Why not?"

"Look, I battle flesh and blood all day long. And that's not the real battle. So, I try to focus my off time on God and my family and friends. I do not want to fall prey to the world. I struggle enough in spiritual warfare that I don't need to invite the bad guys into my thoughts and my home."

Rachel was really confused by what Todd just said. "Spiritual warfare? Like angels and demons and stuff?"

Todd could tell he was losing her. He didn't mean to jump into that full force, but it just came out that way. "Wait here," he said as he left the room. A couple of minutes later he came back with a Bible and a notepad. "Ok, what do you know about angels?"

"Um, they have wings?" Rachel said sarcastically.

"No, I'm being serious. Tell me what you know from the Bible about angels."

"They are messengers."

"Ok," Todd said as he wrote the word on the tablet. "What else?"

"They worship God."

"Ok," Todd kept writing. "And?"

"They don't marry. They don't die."

Todd continued writing. "Right. But most of all, they are spiritual beings. They do not have a fleshy body but can present in human form. Hebrews says angels are ministering spirits sent to serve those who will inherit salvation. The Bible is riddled with examples of angels." Todd's eyes lit up as he started rattling off examples and turning the pages in the Bible to read her passages in Psalms, Isaiah, Luke, Mark, Peter, Colossians, and Revelation. Rachel was fascinated by his command of the Bible and his passion on this subject, even if it was a little strange.

"I guess I never really thought much about it. I didn't realize there were so many references to them in the Bible. I guess I just thought about Michael and Gabriel."

"The writer of Hebrews says the angels are innumerable. And what do you know about Satan?"

"He's a fallen angel."

"Right. He chose to disobey God and took a third of the angels with him. Those are demons. They are his army, and they want nothing more than to destroy us and prevent us from becoming part of God's Kingdom."

"Why do you think they care? I mean, doesn't Satan know that God is all powerful, and he's going to lose in the end?" Rachel asked.

"Sure, he knows. But it doesn't stop him from being jealous," Todd said.

"Of us? I guess I was always jealous of the angels."

Todd smiled and flipped to Corinthians. "Ok, read the first 3 verses. I know you probably have read it before because the passage is about lawsuits among believers, but read it again."

Rachel took the Bible from him and read out loud, "If any of you has a dispute with another, do you dare to take it before the ungodly for judgment instead of before the Lord's people? Or do you not know that the Lord's people will judge the world? And if you are to judge the world, are you not competent to judge trivial cases? Do you not know that we will judge angels? How much more the things of this life!"

Todd asked, "Still jealous of angels?"

Rachel tilted her head to think about that, "Hmm. I had never really thought about us judging the angels. So, do you think Satan is jealous because we will judge them?"

"I think he is jealous that we were created in God's image and are considered higher than the angels. I think that he is jealous of our relationship with God and wants to thwart that at any and every turn." Todd paused and then continued. "Paul says in Ephesians 6 that we wrestle not against flesh and blood, but against principalities, against powers, against the rulers of the darkness of this world, against spiritual wickedness in high places. He's talking about Satan and his demons. They are the rulers of darkness, the principalities we must rid ourselves of."

"Isn't that what the Holy Spirit is for?"

"Well, after we accept Jesus, yes, the Holy Spirit comes to dwell within us to help us become righteous and fight the flesh, but we need the help of angels in this spiritual battle against the demons. Many Christians don't know to call on God's army of angels to help them fight the battles we face."

"Ok, this is a little out there for me," Rachel said.

"Ok, Ok, do you like Chris Tomlin?"

"Yes."

"He's pretty mainstream Christian, right? Well what about his song 'Whom Shall I Fear' – what do you think he's referring to when he talks about the God of angel armies?"

Rachel thought about that for a minute and sang the song in her head. "Ok."

"And what about Billy Graham? He's a good old Baptist preacher, right? He has an entire book on angels."

"Yeah, but do you really believe there is a spiritual battle going on?"

"Yes, I do. Tell me this. Why is it so easy for you to believe that God exists, that Jesus came to earth as a man, died on the cross for your sins and was raised from the dead but so difficult to believe there are angels and demons, especially since there is example after example of them in the text?" Rachel was moved by what Todd said. She was moved by his passion with how he said it, but she was still having trouble processing the information. "Listen, God is a supernatural God. The fact that he raised Jesus from the dead is supernatural. You're not convinced, are you?"

"It's just different. You may have to pray about that for me."

"Rachel, I've been praying for you since the day I met you." Todd realized how stunned Rachel looked. "How about I pray with you?"

Rachel was taken back by the offer. She wasn't sure about praying with Todd. Usually she did that stuff alone or in church with a bunch of other people. "Really?"

"Absolutely." Todd said as he took her hand and started to pray. He thanked God for bringing Rachel into his life, for the abundant blessings God had poured out on him, for his son Jesus, for his mother's hospitality. He asked for forgiveness for where he had fallen short of living his faith, and then asked for God's wisdom and mercy with regard to the box, for physical protection from harm, for healing for Rachel, for Rachel's business to be a beacon in the community, for God to reveal the power of his angel armies to Rachel, for her to know she can rely on Jesus to command the angels to protect her from the demons in this world who seek to distract us from the Kingdom, and for her to be on fire with desire for the Lord so hot that the flames of grace she showed would melt the hearts of those hardened around her so they may come to a saving knowledge of Jesus Christ. It was a long, powerful prayer, and Rachel was overcome with emotion and a true sense of peace by the end of it.

After he was finished, Todd wiped a tear from her cheek. "Tomorrow, then?" he said as he stood and left the room.

Rachel sat on the couch in shock of what just happened. It had been a while since someone else prayed for her in her presence. "Wow," Rachel said under her breath, still feeling as if this whole thing was surreal. She closed her eyes and prayed for God's wisdom to know what to do with this man. She opened her eyes and stared at the open Bible, going over the conversation and prayer in her head again. And again.

Chapter 32

Morning came early to Rachel. Her head had finally stopped pounding from the accident, but she was tired. And Todd would be there soon, she figured. She dragged herself into the shower and then dressed. As she entered the kitchen, she noticed a note on the counter, again indicating that Jimma had left her breakfast. She warmed up the plate and took it to the dining room to eat. She wondered what was so special about that box – or the invitation – that everyone was after it. She wondered about the men at the scene of her accident. Did "red dove" mean something? Or were they good Samaritans just going through her purse to find emergency contact information? Well, they were pretty lousy at it if so, but then again, her phone does have a password on it.

Rachel was deep in thought when Todd entered the house. She missed hearing the door close and was startled when he entered the room.

"Ready to go?" Todd asked.

Rachel dropped her fork at the sound of his voice and jumped in her seat. Her heart raced a couple of beats before she realized it was Todd. She laughed at herself. "Yeah, just let me put this up," she said as she cleared the table. "Where are we going?"

"Jimmy has a CI I thought we might go see."

"A CI?"

"Confidential informant. Someone who gives us information from time to time that is useful for making arrests."

"Oh. I thought those were only real in the movies."

"Well, you don't get many of them who are willing to roll on their buddies, so it's not all that common. My brother has worked in the same precinct for 15 years, though."

"How is this guy going to help us?" Rachel asked.

"I'm not entirely sure he can, but he's pretty knowledgeable about the black market, so maybe he's heard of our art thief or the missing painting."

"Fair enough," Rachel answered. "Let me just get my stuff."

Todd grabbed a drink from the fridge and headed for the car. Rachel followed and waved Todd to the other side of the car. "Partners again, right?"

Todd smiled and caved. "Just this last time."

The Challenger pulled into the parking lot of an older shopping center, anchored by a local auto parts dealer.

A random shopping cart was slowly rolling toward the center of the lot while a man was trying to buckle his toddler into a red Dodge pickup. The light breeze was blowing pieces of trash around the nearly empty lot. Todd parked the car in front of a store labeled "Easy Pawn". The bars on the windows gave Rachel a slight chill.

"Stay here," Todd said.

"Yeah, that's not going to happen," Rachel protested.

Todd rolled his eyes. He didn't want to expose Rachel to any more danger than he had to, but he knew how interested she was in finding out information. "Ok, then let's do what we should have before we left today," Todd said.

"What's that?" Rachel asked.

"Pray for wisdom and protection in our search."

"Ok, will you do it?" Rachel asked, still uncomfortable with praying in front of Todd.

"Absolutely," Todd answered as he grabbed Rachel's hand and prayed out loud.

Todd wrapped up the prayer and got out of the vehicle. The two walked toward the store and entered. The door to the store had a bell on it, making their entry known to all inside. A slender man with dark skin and an unkempt beard emerged from a door behind a glass case at the back of the store. His green army jacket and jeans were tattered a bit. He fidgeted with a watch as he approached the counter. "Something I can do for you?" he asked.

Todd stepped toward the counter. "Yeah, I'm looking for Alfred?"

"Well, you found him," the man said with a smile, revealing his gold front tooth as he proudly beat his chest. "Tell me how Alfred can help you today. You lookin' for some bling for your woman? I got chains, I got rings, I got –"

Todd interrupted and pulled back his shirt to reveal the badge on his belt, "Jimmy sent me."

The man's smile instantly disappeared. "Man, I didn't do nothin'," he said as he shook his head and waved his arm in the air.

"Jimmy said you are the man to see about some art," Todd said.

The man smiled at the thought. His demeanor changed once again. "Yeah? What else did Jimmy say?"

"Are you the man to see or not?" Todd asked.

"Oh yeah, I'm the man, alright. I'm the man," he said proudly beating his chest again.

Todd moved toward the counter. "J.P. Jones. You know him?"

"Yeah, I know him. He got sent up river a while back for capping his old lady."

"Did he try to move any art right before that?"

Alfred backed away from the counter and put his hands up in the air. "Hey, man, I run a legitimate business," he protested.

Todd recognized that Alfred was going to walk a thin line on being an informant, careful not to say too much to get himself into trouble. Todd pulled out a $20 and put it on the counter under his right hand. "You're right, man, you're right. I just want some information. Has J.P. done any business with you lately?" Todd asked, trying to calm Alfred down.

Alfred took the money and put it in his pocket. "Nah, man. He would bring me some stuff from time to time back in the days, but word was he was all dried up, ya know what I mean?" Alfred said with his eyes widened.

Todd was discouraged by the conversation. "Have you seen him around lately?"

"Since he capped his old lady? Nah, man. I ain't gonna let no wife beater do business with me. I got a reputation to consider."

"You heard anything about him wanting to move some art?"

"What do you think this is? Wikipedia or something?" Alfred said in a huff as he backed away from the counter.

Todd paused and stepped back from the counter. He grabbed Rachel's hand and started walking toward the door. "Jimmy said if something moved in this town, you knew about it. I guess he was wrong about that."

"What do you mean he was wrong? This is my town. Ain't nothin' gonna move in this town without me knowing about it!" Alfred yelled out and then muttered under his breath, "No cop gonna tell me I don't know what's happening in my own town."

Todd stopped and turned back toward Alfred. "Are you sure nothing moves in this town without you knowing about it?"

"Yeah, man, I'm sure. You can just keep on walking," Alfred said.

Todd smiled, "Has J.P. tried to move something or not?"

"I wouldn't tell you if he had," Alfred said.

Todd scanned the shop for a minute and focused his eyes on a stack of Blue Ray player boxes on a shelf to his right. "You know, Alfred, I think Best Buy may have reported a burglary a few days ago."

Alfred moved in front of the boxes. "No, man, I bought those outright. They ain't hot, man, I'm telling you. They ain't hot."

"Did I say they were?" Todd turned to Rachel and asked her, "Did I say these Blue Ray players were hot?"

"Come on, man. They ain't hot. I swear on my grandmomma's grave they ain't hot, ok," Alfred said.

Todd smiled, "I'll just need to get my boys down here to haul them to the station and run the serial numbers through our database, just to clear you. Shouldn't take but a couple of weeks, maybe a month," Todd said back.

"Come on, man. I move 15 of those a week. You can't just take my stuff. I got receipts!" Alfred said.

"Did J.P. try to move anything or not?" Todd asked again.

Alfred stared at him. "Those ain't hot, man. I got a guy in Nashville. They are legit."

Todd didn't flinch.

Alfred caved, "Ok, Ok, I heard he might get something rare he wanted to move, but he never came through."

"Rare like what?"

"I dunno, man. Something small, but worth a whole lotta cheese."

"How much?"

"Six zeros."

"Who did he make the deal with, Alfred?"

"I don't know who the deal was with, I swear."

Todd didn't flinch. The two stared at each other for a few seconds.

"You gotta give me something, Alfred."

"Come on, man, I got a reputation to protect." Alfred said.

Todd moved toward the boxes of players. Alfred blurted out, "Ok, Ok, all I know is that J.P. is staying at the Moon Shadow Motel in Horn Lake." Alfred paused. "That's all I know, man, I swear."

Todd stared at Alfred for a minute and decided that was all he was going to get. "Pleasure doing business with you, Alfred."

"Yeah, you tell Jimmy he owes me," Alfred said as Todd and Rachel walked out. "You tell him he owes me, you hear?" Alfred shouted as the door closed.

Rachel could feel the adrenaline pumping as they got back into the Challenger. She had a huge smile on her face. "That was so cool!" she said.

Todd started the engine and chuckled. "Liked that, did you?"

"Yeah," Rachel said. "Think those Blue Ray players are really stolen?"

"Nah, Jimmy says he's pretty careful. He wouldn't put that stuff on his shelf out in the open like that if they were hot. But the threat of tying them up for weeks on end sure made him squeal." Todd pulled out of the parking lot. "Hey, can you find the address for that motel on my phone?" Todd asked as he tossed her his phone.

"Sure," Rachel said as she started punching letters on the keyboard. "Looks like it's right off 51 on Church Street."

"Near the college?" Todd asked.

"Yeah, two blocks from it." Rachel put the phone down and thought about the conversation in the pawn shop. She stared out the window and wondered what J.P. was trying to sell. Was it the box? Was it worth that much?

"Will you hand me my phone, please?" Todd asked. Rachel did as she was asked and Todd punched up his contacts and pushed a button. Rachel could see on the screen that he was calling Jimmy.

"Hey, it's Todd," Todd started. Rachel could only hear his end of the call. "We just left there. Alfred claims there was a deal on the table with Esther, but he says he didn't know who it was with or what the deal was." Silence. "Yeah." Todd paused for a while as he listened. "I know." Short pause. "Anything on Rachel's apartment?" Silence. "I know, but –" More silence. "But there has to be something –" Todd stopped again. "That's not a lot of good choices." Todd paused again. "Yeah, ok. Later." Todd hung up the phone.

"Your brother?" Rachel asked.

"Yeah," Todd said, visibly rattled by the call.

"Let me guess. They didn't find any leads on my apartment?" Rachel asked.

"No, I'm sorry. They didn't." Todd pulled the car to the side of the road and turned to face Rachel. "And I know what you are going to say, but I don't want you to go with me to see J.P. I'm afraid this thing might spiral out of control."

Rachel started to protest, and then she looked Todd in the eyes and saw the concern on his face. She stopped herself and caved. "Ok."

"Ok?" Todd repeated, confused.

"Yeah," Rachel said with the sound of defeat in her voice. Todd smiled at her. Rachel had a thought – maybe they were going about this all wrong. "If you take Jimmy with you. And hey, will you drop me by your mom's country club before you head to Horn Lake?"

Todd was happy she didn't want to force going to see J.P. "Sure. Ma should be there by now."

Chapter 33

As the Challenger pulled into the lot, Rachel noticed two exotic cars and many that would cost more than she would ever spend on a car. Todd pulled under the covered parking and she started to exit the car. "You going to be ok with this? Those women are something else," Todd said.

Rachel smiled and said, "I can handle it."

"No doubt. Dinner tonight?"

"Officer Henderson, are you asking me out on a date?"

"I'm asking if you want to eat dinner with me. The word 'date' never came out of my mouth," Todd said through a smile.

Rachel couldn't help herself. "In that case, I'd love to. Pick me up here after you get through with J.P."

Rachel felt the rush of adrenaline from flirting with Todd. Once she entered the club, it didn't take long for Jimma to spot her and come running. "Come, dear, I have some friends I want you to meet!" Jimma said. Rachel was surprised to see Jimma in such a colorful outfit, complete with heavy costume jewelry and a sun hat. She had transformed into a lady of leisure, Rachel thought. Jimma pulled Rachel toward a group of women similarly dressed sipping tea and playing Mahjong at a table in the corner. It was just as Rachel imagined it would be. "Ladies, this is Rachel. Rachel, meet Grace, Sue, Patricia and Barbara."

"Nice to meet you, ladies," Rachel said with a smile. She stuck her hand out to shake, only to realize that was not the appropriate gesture. She tried to cover it up by pulling her purse strap firmly onto her shoulder.

"Rachel, now tell us all about you and Todd. Jimma here refuses to share anything," Sue said as she looked Rachel up and down.

"Oh, stop it, Sue. Leave the girl alone," Grace said as she slapped Sue's hand.

"What? I'm just sayin' what all y'all are thinking," Sue protested.

Patricia chimed in, "Rachel, don't you tell her a thing. She's just old an old woman looking for some juicy gossip."

The ladies all started to argue amongst themselves about whether or not they should try to get details from Rachel while Jimma put her hands over her face in embarrassment.

Rachel interrupted their chatter to say, "Well, there's nothing really to tell."

Silence fell in the room. "What?" Sue asked. "Nothing to tell? You mean you are just stringing that boy along?"

"Sue!" Grace shouted in disapproval.

Sue snapped, "What? You know that boy is madly in love with her. Why, he'd go to the moon and back for her. I just think she ought to have sense enough to recognize a good man when she sees one, is all I'm sayin'."

"Ladies," Jimma interrupted, "Todd and Rachel are friends, getting to know one another right now. Let's leave it at that."

Sue started to protest, but Grace knocked one of her pieces off the board and into the floor. Sue leaned down to get it and said, "Grace Howard! How dare you try to cheat like that!"

Grace motioned for Jimma and Rachel to go before Sue popped her head back up. Jimma took the que and pushed Rachel into the next room. "Oh, I'm sorry about that, honey. Sometimes these ladies look for any gossip they can find."

"Well, I can assure you I wouldn't have come if I couldn't handle a few ladies asking questions about my love life," Rachel said with a smile.

Jimma smiled back. She liked Rachel. "Then you've come to the right place. There will be lots more where that came from, I can tell you that right now."

"Speaking of gossip, you said that there was a lot of it surrounding J.P. and Esther's non-wedding?" Rachel asked.

"Oh yeah, everyone here had their own theory about what happened to that poor girl," Jimma said. "Not finding her body just fueled those fires."

"Did Mary come here often?"

"Her mom? Nearly every day."

"Did she have a favorite spot?"

"She sat out on the terrace and watched the golfers a lot."

"Great. Jimma, will you excuse me?"

"Sure, sweetie, but –" Jimma's words trailed off as Rachel made her way to the back of the club in search of the terrace.

Rachel rounded the corner and found a place to sit. She could see why Mary liked the terrace. The chairs had nice padding and a strong back support for outdoor chairs. The area was protected by a very high outdoor ceiling with lights and fans. She could see the entire first hole from where she sat, but the traffic in and out of the course was on the other side of the terrace. Rachel imagined she was facing a direction that either had a great view of the sunrise or the sunset, but she wasn't sure which one. Rachel waited for the server to come to her table and ordered a Coke. When the server returned, Rachel asked, "Did you know Mary Adams?"

"Frozen face? Yeah, I knew her. I'm sorry the old lady is dead, but she never did me any favors, ya know? She would only let Emma serve her, like the rest of us had cooties or something," the girl said as she put the Coke down. "You need anything else, hun?"

"Is Emma here?" Rachel asked.

"Yeah, she's not on the clock yet. You wanna talk to her? I can ask her to come over here."

"Yes, please," Rachel said.

A young girl Rachel imagined to be about 19 approached the table.

"Emma?" Rachel asked.

"Yes, ma'am. Heather said you wanted to see me."

"Do you have time to sit for a minute and talk to me?"

"Ok, sure," the girl answered as she pulled out a chair and sat opposite of Rachel.

"Emma, I wanted to ask you about Mary Adams. I bought her house and had a few questions about her. Heather said she would only let you serve her."

"Yes, ma'am. She rubbed some people the wrong way, but she was a nice lady. I think she was just misunderstood. You know, some people are just that way, but I don't think you should hold that against them," Emma started. She was a talker for sure, Rachel thought.

"What do you mean by 'that way'?"

"Well, she had little quirks that other people made fun of, but I knew it was just her way of coping with things."

"What do you mean by quirks?"

"Like she was short with people. She was specific about what she ordered and gave people a hard time if they messed it up, but really all you had to do was listen to get it right. I didn't think it was that hard. And, she brought her own condiments and pulled them out of this giant purse she carried. A lot of people thought that was strange, but it didn't bother me. She always wore a hat and smelled like moth balls which reminded me of my grandmother. But Heather was so mean to her. She called her 'frozen face' because Ms. Adams didn't smile much, but I think she was just sad and lonely. Oh, and she wore the same blouse a lot. She told me it was the last thing her son gave her before they had a big fight, so she liked to wear it to be close to him. She was hoping he'd come to visit her, and she'd be wearing the blouse. I figured that's why she held onto that invitation so tight every day as well."

"Invitation? To the wedding?"

"Yeah, she used to talk about her son coming to the ceremony."

"Did she bring the invitation with her a lot?"

"Every day for a couple of months before the wedding. The servers were really mean about it, making fun of her for carrying it around. They said if she wasn't so mean that someone would actually come visit her. She'd just sit here and stare at it all day. It was so sad to me. And then one day, she didn't bring it anymore."

"Did you ask her about it?"

"Yeah, she told me that Esther told her to put it in a safe place."

"Why?"

"I don't know. She had kind of gotten paranoid by then. She said Esther told her if anyone found out she had it, she'd be in danger."

"The invitation?"

"Yeah, but like I said, she was paranoid and acting weird by then."

"Thank you, Emma. I appreciate you talking to me."

Emma stood to leave and turned back just as she was walking away. "Ms. Adams seemed to really regret not being able to see her son. If you talk to him, will you let him know that she loved him? I think it would mean a lot to her."

"Absolutely, Emma." Rachel thought about their conversation and wondered what was so special about that invitation or if it was just the paranoia from an old lady. Maybe none of this was connected to her in any way. After all, they hadn't really been able to establish a connection with J.P. and the box.

Chapter 34

Rachel decided she needed to focus her attention on work for a while. She pulled out her computer and began working. She traded several emails with Sara about work, and of course about her sleeping arrangements at Jimma's, the box and Todd. Finally, Rachel called Sara.

"It's not a game, Sara. I need to solve this."

"Why? Can't you just give the box to the FBI or something. We have lives, ya know? We have a business to run. You can't chase ghosts forever."

"I know, Sara, and I'm sorry I haven't been to the office this week. Everything on my projects is under control. And I promise I'll come back in next week, whether or not this thing is wrapped up."

"Promise?"

"Promise."

"Ok, so I still think he's all wrong for you and a total weirdo, but have you kissed him yet?"

"Sara!"

"Come on, Rachel. You owe me something!"

"Um, well, we are going to dinner tonight."

"And?"

"And, I know I said I don't date cops, but –"

"I knew it! I knew you'd go to his mom's, and they would suck you into this weird fantasy."

"What? No, it's not...oh, never mind. I have work to do. Look, just keep the fort down with Preston, and we'll work on the Medtec RFP on Monday."

"Fine. Enjoy your date!" Sara said in a huff. Rachel put the phone down and plowed through her work. She hoped that Sara would understand.

Patricia, one of the ladies from earlier, made her way to the terrace and waved at Rachel as she made her way toward her. "Oh, I don't mean to intrude, but can I sit with you for a minute?"

Rachel motioned for her to sit and said, "Of course. I'm just finishing up."

"I just love to have an afternoon snack on the terrace when the weather is nice. Don't you?"

"It is nice out here today with the fans going," Rachel said.

"Have you made up your mind yet, child?" Patricia asked.

"Oh, no, I can't eat anymore right now," Rachel said.

"No, that's not what I meant," Patricia waved the server down and asked for a slice of apple pie and a coffee. "I mean about Jimma's boy. Have you made up your mind about him yet? That is why you are here, isn't it?"

"Oh, we are just friends," Rachel insisted.

"Friends? What does that even mean? I don't understand you young people with your need to wait to get married. In my day, you met a nice boy, you went out on a few dates, and you married. And you stayed married. Nowadays everyone wants to fall in love," Patricia lectured, "like being 'in love' is a thing. Love is an action word. If you want to know how to find the right one, you be the right one. You love first and always. You don't live with someone first to try it out, you jump head first into a real commitment with no life preserver. That's what's wrong with marriages these days. It's too easy to get out of them with these quickie divorces."

Rachel was a little taken back by the lecture. "What about your husband, Patricia? How did y'all meet?"

"Oh, like everyone else my age. We went to high school together. I suppose it was easier back then. The pool of available men was smaller. Less for us to choose from. And we didn't go anywhere unless a man asked us, so we were motivated to find a man and hang on to him," Patricia said.

The server brought out Patricia's pie and coffee. "Oh, don't mind me, honey, I am just an old woman," Patricia said.

Rachel smiled as she thought about Patricia's words. They may have sounded old fashioned, but there was a lot of wisdom in them. "I don't think so. I think you are a wise woman," Rachel said.

"Well, then you tell me about Jimma's boy. You like him?" Patricia said.

"Yes, ma'am, I do," Rachel answered.

"Now that's what I like to hear. You just need to say that in front of the pastor, and you are all set," Patricia smiled as she stabbed her apple pie with a fork.

Rachel should have seen that one coming. "I don't think we are quite there yet, Ms. Patricia."

"Well, you aren't going to find a better man than Todd. He is a gem, that one is. And boy does he like you," Patricia said as she put a bit in her mouth.

Rachel blushed. "He doesn't know me very well yet, though."

"Nonsense. Do you know Jesus?" Patricia asked.

Rachel was confused. "Yes," she answered hesitantly.

"Well, that's all he needs to know. If the two of you put Jesus first in your life, the rest will take care of itself. Ask Jimma. She's living proof," Patricia said.

"How so?" Rachel asked.

"You don't know? Jimma and Michael met on a mission trip when they were 17. They got married two weeks later. They didn't have anything in common except Jesus, and they were happily married for what would have been 40 years if it hadn't been for his accident in South America."

Rachel tried to take all that in. "His accident? He didn't get killed in the line of duty?"

"Oh, sure he did, just not as a cop. He was on duty as a missionary in South America when a building collapsed. Michael ran back in to help. He saved eight people that day including Todd and Jimmy. It was that last sweep of the building that got him. He felt he had to go one more time to make sure everyone was out, but the building wasn't stable enough, and it collapsed on him."

Rachel was shocked to hear the story. She let it settle for a minute. All this time she thought Michael had been killed as a cop, not as a missionary. But Todd had literally watched his father die in front of him, while he was saving other people, giving his own life for his sons and others. She couldn't imagine what that must be like. They probably had to dig his body out. Suddenly her sad story about her dad leaving at age six seemed like a picnic compared to what Todd had been through. Tears flooded her eyes and started to fall.

Patricia reached out and grabbed her hand. "Oh, honey, I didn't mean to upset you."

Rachel tried to compose herself. "I didn't know," Rachel said.

Just then, Todd showed up, and Rachel began packing up her things. "How did you survive with the ladies? Did they torture you for information about us?"

"Us?" Rachel teased.

"You know what I mean," Todd said.

"Yeah, actually I didn't get in the door good before they gave me a grilling, but nothing I can't handle," Rachel said. "Hey, what did you find out?"

"Unfortunately, nothing. J.P. hadn't been there in a few days."

"Seriously?' Rachel said as she slammed her computer into her bag. She pulled her hand up to her forehead and rubbed it. Todd moved toward her and put his arm around her. "Are we ever going to solve this?" she asked Todd.

"It does seem like one step forward, one step back, but that's really how these things go sometimes." Todd said. "Let's just enjoy the evening."

"What about your mom?"

"I talked to her earlier. We are going to have dessert at her house later."

"Todd, I really feel like I'm intruding on her. It's been like 4 days. I need to go home."

Todd chuckled. "Yeah, like that's going to happen. Not until we wrap this up. Plus, my mom is loving every second of this. I mean it. She's in hog heaven. Don't take her joy away!"

Rachel wasn't sure what to do. She felt like she was imposing, but Todd made it sound like Jimma needed her company. "Ok, but just for a couple more days, and then I have to go home. I promised Sara I'd be back in the office on Monday."

Todd grabbed her bag from her and headed toward the door. Rachel followed and let her mind wonder again what it would be like to kiss Todd.

Chapter 35

Dinner was at the Maria's Italian Kitchen. Rachel loved Italian food, but she found it difficult to eat politely on a date. She didn't like to wrap noodles on a fork like you were supposed to. She preferred to cut it up to avoid any string mishaps that left uneaten noodles lingering on her chin. But that wasn't proper etiquette. Still, she was who she was, and pretending to eat pasta in an awkward way to impress someone wasn't her style. She argued with herself about it, and then decided to avoid the problem altogether by ordering lasagna.

"So, what was going on between you and Patricia back there? It looked pretty intense," Todd asked.

"It was," Rachel said and paused. "She kind of, um, accidentally, um, told me about your dad's accident," Rachel admitted.

"It's not a secret or anything, Rachel," Todd said, almost nonchalant about it.

"It's a big deal, though, Todd."

"Yeah, it is. My dad was a hero."

"And you aren't mad at God?"

"Why would I be mad at God? Don't get me wrong. I loved my dad, and I miss him every day, and yes, I wish he were still with us, but this place is not our home. We are temporary. Here for a purpose. And my dad fulfilled that purpose in the greatest way. He lived so much for Jesus that he was ready to be called home at any time."

Rachel's trouble processing that was obvious to Todd.

"Look, Rachel, my dad died telling people about Jesus as he was saving them. It was incredible," Todd said. "I can't think of a better call to homecoming than that."

Rachel couldn't believe that this man wanted to be with her. He was so much more spiritually mature than she ever hoped to be. He was special. She couldn't contain the smile that came across her face. She wanted to jump up and shout out loud how incredible this man was. Fortunately, the server appeared with their food before she made any such motions.

Todd had ordered spaghetti, and twirled it properly on his fork, much to Rachel's dismay. However, a noodle mishap caught her attention, and they both laughed as a noodle stuck to Todd's chin. Todd quickly grabbed his napkin and took care of the situation, but not before the embarrassment kicked in.

"I have to be honest. I don't eat pasta this way, normally. At home, I cut it up to avoid what you just saw," Todd started.

"Oh, but it was such a great show!" Rachel teased, and then she felt the need to rescue him. "If we are being totally honest, I didn't order the spaghetti for the exact same reason."

They both enjoyed another laugh, and Todd picked up his knife. "Ok, then, I'm cutting. I mean, really, who thought wrapping slippery noodles on a fork was a good idea?"

"Yeah, apparently, Emily Post never had to do it on a date!"

Todd stopped laughing. And then Rachel realized what she said. Todd smiled and continued cutting his spaghetti.

"So, do you think I can have your actual number now?"

Rachel had almost forgotten that she never corrected the mistake. "Give me your phone." Todd handed her his phone. Rachel stood up and walked around the table just behind Todd. She crouched down and held the phone out. Todd smiled as Rachel leaned her head toward his. She snapped the perfect picture of the two of them smiling and walked back to her seat without a word. She punched in her numbers and used the picture as her contact icon. She passed the phone back to Todd and grinned. Todd couldn't have been more pleased at her response. She was starting to see them together.

Chapter 36

Todd and Rachel entered the house laughing and holding hands. It was a sight that Jimma had been hoping to see for a while. She pretended not to notice as she closed the door behind them. "I've got chocolate cake in the kitchen. Y'all go on into the den, and I'll bring it in."

Rachel was immediately self-conscious about holding Todd's hand and dropped it. Jimma went to the kitchen and started working. She dropped a plate a little hard on the counter, and Rachel decided to go see how she could help. "You alright, Jimma?"

"Well, I am now. Took you long enough."

"Oh, I'm sorry, Jimma. I should have come in to help earlier."

"Not about that, dear. The kitchen I can handle. I mean about giving my boy a chance to win your heart."

Rachel was embarrassed and looked down at the floor. "Jimma, we were just –"

"Holding hands, I know, child," Jimma said sarcastically as she grabbed Rachel's face and pulled it upward to look her in the eyes. Her tone turned serious and loving, "But I can see it in your eyes. I can hear it in your laughter."

Rachel's eyes filled with tears. "I don't want to hurt him, Jimma."

Jimma pulled Rachel into a hug. "Oh, honey, sometimes getting hurt is part of life. Todd is a big boy. He can handle it. I know you are scared about him being a cop. Take your time, but trust me when I tell you, this is worth pursuing." Jimma paused. Rachel swallowed back her tears. "Besides, any man who will help you escape from a hospital has to be worth something, right?"

Rachel and Jimma started laughing. Todd entered the kitchen. "What kind of trouble am I interrupting in here?"

"No trouble. Just cutting the cake," Jimma said.

"Oh, anytime women are giggling in the kitchen there is trouble," Todd said.

"We're just enjoying ourselves, honey," Jimma said as she handed Todd a piece of cake. The three of them finished their cake standing in the kitchen talking. After they finished, they all pitched in to clean up the kitchen. "There. Now you two go enjoy yourselves. I've got some calls to make."

Rachel and Todd entered the den and sat on the couch. "This is becoming a habit," Todd said.

"You complaining?" Rachel asked jokingly.

"Never," Todd said with a smile.

Rachel clasped her hands around Todd's. "If I didn't know better, I'd think you were dragging out this investigation to keep me here."

"Well, I can't say I'm upset about the arrangements," Todd said with a smile.

"Your mom is so great," Rachel said.

"You aren't so bad yourself," Todd said.

Rachel blushed with embarrassment and looked down at their hands. She felt her heart racing slightly. Todd could see how uncomfortable Rachel was. "Well, I've got an early shift tomorrow. I'll swing by about 4? We can go check on your car and go from there?"

Rachel nodded in agreement as Todd stood up to leave. Rachel let his hand go slowly. She wanted him to stay, but she knew she should let him go. Todd leaned back down. He wanted to kiss Rachel passionately but opted for a peck on the cheek. "I'll see you tomorrow," he whispered in her ear and left before she had a chance to respond. Rachel heard a "Bye Ma," as Todd closed the door.

Rachel sank back against the couch and closed her eyes to enjoy the moment, but her phone started buzzing again. She looked down to see an email from one of her clients. He wanted to meet tomorrow at 9 to discuss a new project. Rachel didn't have a car. She hated to let this client down; it was one of her oldest and best clients. Maybe she could rent a car?

Jimma entered the room and saw Rachel frantically pushing buttons on her phone. "Something wrong, sweetie?"

"I'm trying to rent a car while mine is in the shop, but this website won't take my credit card information," Rachel said while pushing harder on the phone as if pressure was going to correct the error on the website.

"Oh, sweetie, don't do that. Michael's truck never gets driven. It's in the garage. You can use that until yours is fixed."

"Oh, no, I couldn't, Jimma. You've done so much for me already. I've got the reservation if I can just get it to go through," Rachel said still staring at the phone and pushing buttons.

Jimma disappeared and then reappeared within a few seconds holding keys in her hand. "Now you cancel that reservation right now, Missy. There is no sense in spending money on a rental car when I have a perfectly good truck sitting in the garage."

Rachel looked up almost in shock, speechless. "I – I –"

"I, nothing. You cancel that reservation."

Rachel started to protest, "But-"

"It's done, Rachel. You will use Michael's truck, and that's the end of it," Jimma said firmly.

Rachel put the phone down and stood up to meet Jimma. "Thank you, Jimma," she said as she moved toward her and took the keys.

Jimma grabbed Rachel's hand and squeezed as she said, "Now was that so hard?"

Rachel smiled. Jimma released her hands and started toward the door. "I'm going to bed. If you need anything else, you know where it is."

"Good night, Jimma."

Rachel tapped out a reply email agreeing to meet her client at 9 and copied Sara before heading to the bedroom. She read her daily devotion and once again found herself distracted by the events of the day. She prayed for God to reveal His plan to her regarding Todd.

Chapter 37

Rachel left the appointment at 10:20 in Bartlett and climbed into the black F150 that had belonged to Todd's dad. She hadn't driven a truck in a while and forgot what it was like to sit up high in a vehicle. She was thankful for the loan. Rachel checked her watch and started out the window for a minute. She wondered what time an early shift was at the police station. Rachel pulled out of the parking lot and headed toward the precinct. She decided to stop at a local sandwich shop and pick up lunch, just in case she could catch Todd.

As she pulled into the precinct, she wasn't sure where to park. She had been with Todd the time before and followed him into the building. She rounded the corner and saw the signs for visitor parking. She parked and started into the building with lunch in her hands. She had a huge smile on her face at the thought of surprising Todd. She hoped that she would get to see him.

Rachel entered the front door and had to go through metal detectors. She placed the sandwich sack on the belt along with her purse and slide it through. She put her keys and phone in a side bowl and grabbed them after emerging from the machine. She grabbed her things and looked for a front desk. There was a line waiting to see the officers at the front counter. She turned and asked the attendant at the metal detector if he could tell her where to go to find Todd Henderson. The officer was busy and pointed to the back of the hall. Go straight and turn left at the end of the hall. Brock Harris can help you locate him.

Rachel did as the officer told her and headed down the hall. She turned left and immediately saw the buzz of officers working frantically to answer phones and do paperwork. She hoped the Brock would remember her. She approached the desk and before she could speak, Brock picked up the phone to call Todd.

"Hey, Henderson, your lady friend is here," he said. Rachel blushed at the mention but was pleased that Brock remembered her. "Yep, sure will," he said as he hung up the phone. His attention turned back to Rachel. "He's on Front Street, heading back this way. He'll be here in a couple of minutes."

"I hope I'm not intruding," Rachel said.

Brock laughed and looked over his shoulder, "Hey, Mason!" he yelled out.

"Yeah?" Mason yelled back.

"Henderson's lady wants to make sure she's not intruding."

Several howls came from around the precinct as three or four officers walked toward Rachel.

Mason emerged from behind a door. He was an older gentleman sporting a gray goatee and short hair. He towered over the others in the office with his commanding height. Mason looked at Rachel and said, "Is that right, now?"

"Yeah," Brock said.

"Oh, I'd say she's intruding alright. I think Henderson has been holding out on us," he said to Brock and then turned to Rachel. "What's your name?"

"Rachel," she answered.

"It's nice to meet you, Rachel. I'm Mason," Mason said. He turned to all the officers who had their attention on Rachel and waved them off. "Tell me, what did Todd do to warrant a visit today?"

Rachel smiled. "I didn't mean to stir up trouble. I just thought it would be nice to have lunch with Todd if he is available."

The crowd of officers made noises in the background making fun of Rachel and Todd having lunch together. Rachel saw one of them making kissing gestures and was a little embarrassed by the suggestion but remembered what Todd had told her before they came on Monday. She knew she'd have to have tougher skin if she was going to continue going out with Todd.

Instead of looking down as was her instinct, she held her head high as if she didn't hear them.

Mason chuckled. "Oh, don't let these guys get to you," he said as he turned back to them and made a serious effort to get them to leave Rachel alone. He said loudly for them all to hear, "They are all just jealous that Henderson has such a beautiful woman coming to meet him at the precinct."

Rachel smiled. "Thank you, Mason. It's nice to meet you."

Mason gestured toward his office. "I'm going for some coffee. If you'd like, you can sit in my office while you wait. Can I get you anything?"

"Oh, no, thank you," Rachel answered.

"Well, make yourself at home. Todd will be along shortly."

Rachel walked into Mason's office and sat in the leather chair facing the desk. She wasn't sure why Mason had an office, as she was sure he wasn't the captain. She looked around the room at the plaques and trophies. Mason had several University of Tennessee items scattered around his office. She figured he got a lot of teasing from the others about rooting for Tennessee so he must be used to their shenanigans. She decided to look busy and pulled her phone out to check something, anything that would make her look less desperate.

Rachel was startled by the noise in the other room as Todd entered the precinct. The other officers were clearly interested in teasing Todd about her presence. She immediately regretting coming and hoped that Todd would not be annoyed with her for surprising him. She stood and walked to the door of Mason's office and almost bumped heads with Todd as he was walking toward her. An awkward "Oh," came out of both of their mouths and then laughter.

Rachel started first, "I'm sorry – I thought you might want some lunch, but I shouldn't have –"

"I'm glad you did," Todd said. "I've only got a few minutes, though, so lunch might have to wait until dinner."

"Oh, I brought lunch with me. Is that ok?" Rachel asked.

Todd smiled. "Perfect! Come with me," Todd said as he pulled Rachel through the precinct to a break room. They sat in the corner, and Rachel pulled the food out of her bag. Todd got two Coca-Colas from the vending machines.

"Roast beef or Chicken?" Rachel asked.

Todd shrugged, "Your choice."

Rachel tossed the Roast beef to Todd's side of the table, and they started to eat. "So how did you get down here?"

Rachel smiled. "Your mother let me borrow your dad's truck until my car is fixed."

"Oh, that's great. It doesn't handle well in the rain, though, so be careful tomorrow. I think we are under a thunderstorm warning in the afternoon."

"Got it. So how long have you been here today?" Rachel asked.

"Since about 4. It's a terrible shift, but everyone has to take it once in a while," Todd said. "Gives me an extra evening free, though."

Rachel smiled and wondered what type of quality evening that left if he had to get up so early. "And what exactly were you planning to do with that extra evening?"

"Well, I thought I might honor my promise to a certain lady about another ride down a quarter mile racetrack, but I guess we have more pressing things to concern ourselves with these days."

Rachel smiled at the thought of going back to the races. "You aren't putting your car back on that track. We are racing mine next time."

"Yours?" Todd asked.

"Uh, yeah. We have to see if its Mopar or who's behind the wheel."

Todd laughed. "Well, I'm not racing a Ford. That might have been my daddy's choice, but nothing beats a Hemi."

Rachel laughed. "You want something done right, you just gotta do it yourself," Rachel teased.

"Oh no, you didn't!" Todd said.

"Yeah, I did," Rachel laughed back and the two of them locked eyes on one another for a brief moment. Then Rachel said, "I've been thinking I'm missing something about the box. Do you think we can look at it again?"

"Sure," Todd answered. "Let me ask Brock to pull it," he said as he left the room for less than two minutes. "Ok, he'll have it in a couple of minutes. What are you thinking?"

"I'm not sure, but something is nagging me about it."

After they finished lunch, Todd retrieved the box from Brock and handed it to Rachel. "How did you open this again?" she asked as she handed it back.

Todd pushed on the opposite ends and popped the secret compartment open. He handed it back to Rachel who let the invitation slide out onto her lap. She studied the outside of it, which was addressed to Mary Adams. There didn't appear to be anything of interest on the outside. She slowly opened the invitation up to study the insert. She read the words three times, looking for any clue. Nothing stood out. She handed it to Todd, frustrated. "See anything interesting?"

Todd took the envelope and invitation from Rachel. "No, just an invitation. Maybe there isn't anything here, and the two break-ins are a coincidence."

Suddenly a knock came at the door frame. "We gotta roll," a voice said in a hurry. Rachel turned around to see Marcus walking past the doorway.

"I'm sorry, Rachel. Just give it back to Brock, and he can put it back, ok? I'll see you tonight. Thanks for lunch!" Todd said as he handed her the invitation and started out the door.

Rachel shouted, "Be careful," and then thought about how silly that must sound. She turned her attention back to the invitation and noticed there was still something in the envelope. She turned it upside down and another envelope fell out. She reached for the envelope and turned it over to reveal a stamp with a red dove on it. "Bingo!" she said as she held it up.

Could this be it? She began thinking about the events of the past few days. Marty Adams said J.P. was into art, stamps, coins, or something like that and because Esther was a painter, and she assumed it was a painting. But then Alfred said it was small, maybe he meant like a postage stamp. Emma at the club said Mary would bring the invitation in every day until Esther told her to hide it or she'd get into trouble. And the guys at the accident were saying 'red dove'. Rachel started tapping frantically on her phone to try to find out anything about the red dove stamp. She began reading, "The red dove is a US postage stamp from 1912 that occurred with an error in the black printing plate. The error was caught early and only a handful of stamps were produced. A postal worker is rumored to have stolen a stamp that was scheduled for destruction. Because it

221

was never circulated and has never been on public display, many do not believe the stamp exists. However, the stamp holds a high value in many circles of the philatelic community as the holy grail of stamps."

Rachel wondered if the stamp was real. She knew Esther was a master artist and thought perhaps it was counterfeit. She tapped on her phone to find out who could appraise a stamp and sorted the options to locate a stamp appraiser on Raleigh-LaGrange Road, which appeared to be the only one in the tri-state area. She quickly collected her trash from lunch, put it away and headed out the door with the box in one hand and the invitation in her purse. Mason passed her in the hallway, "You gone, pretty lady?"

Rachel was slightly flustered with a thousand thoughts in her head. "Yeah, I've got to, um, I'm going to see a, uh, um guy about a stamp."

Mason had a strange look on his face, "A stamp? Ok, then. You enjoy yourself. Hope these guys didn't scare you off."

"Oh, no, I just need to go. Thank you for letting me use your office," Rachel said as she continued walking down the hall.

"Anytime, anytime," Mason said as he went about his business.

Rachel handed the box to Brock as she left. "Thank you," she said, "I'll bring back the invitation after I check out this stamp."

Chapter 38

Rachel climbed into the truck and put her phone on the dashboard to show her directions. She headed toward the stamp collector's business and tried to work everything out in her head. If the stamp was fake, then why was everyone looking for it? Maybe they didn't know it was fake? Or maybe it was real? She was just wasting her thoughts. She needed to know for sure. She turned the radio on and tried to sing along to engage her brain in something other than this circular thought process that wasn't productive.

Rachel pulled into the gravel lot and checked the address. She entered the building labeled GH Collectibles. The door chimed as she entered and an older gentleman with a soft voice greeted her. "Welcome to GH Collectibles. What can I do for you today?"

"Well, I'm looking for the value of a stamp," Rachel said.

"Oh sure. Do you have insurance papers with you? I will need to fill those out for you if you expect the appraisal to stand," the man said.

"No, I'm not looking for an insurance appraisal. I just need to see if the stamp is worth anything or not," Rachel asked. "How much do you charge for your services?"

"$50," the man said. "But I don't take checks anymore. I've had too many of those burn me in the past."

Rachel dug into her purse and found some cash. "$50."

The man slowly rung up the transaction on his antique-looking machine, put the money in the drawer meticulously and handed Rachel a receipt. "Well, let's see this stamp of yours."

Rachel pulled the RSVP envelope out of the invitation and handed it to the man. His eyes grew wide, and Rachel could tell that he knew right away all about the legend of the red dove stamp. He cleared his throat and tried to pretend he was not rattled by its presence. He pulled out his microscope and placed the envelope under it. He twisted the lens and began looking through it at the stamp as he talked. "Where did you get this?" he asked.

"I just came into it recently," Rachel said.

"You know, a lot of people leave this sort of thing to their kin and don't leave any instructions," he looked up from the microscope and stared at Rachel, "Of course, that has helped me make a living for many years, so I can't complain." He looked back down into the lens, "It is odd that someone placed it onto this envelope. It's a good thing no one mailed this." The man looked up

224

from the microscope and said, "I need to run an acid test on it in the back where some of my equipment is. It will just take a few minutes."

The man disappeared into the back room leaving Rachel alone in the store. She looked around at the odd collection in the store and thought how strange it is that people find value in the things in his store. She picked up a snow globe of Memphis with Graceland in it and shook it. She smiled as she watched the music notes and snow trickle back down around the Cadillac in the globe. Suddenly, she felt a hard blow to the head. She dropped the snow globe and fell next to it. Everything went black.

Chapter 39

Rachel slowly opened her eyes. Her hands were tied to the chair arms with duct tape and her mouth gagged with a bandana. She slung her feet to realize they were also attached to the chair legs. She looked around at the room she was in. It was full of boxes. She tried to read the labels on the boxes around her, but she could only make out the word "Collectibles". She must be in the warehouse for GH Collectibles. She tried to yell out, but the gag muted the sound. She tugged at her wrists and her feet to no avail. Her head throbbed from the hit on the head and her neck was stiff. At least it wasn't pitch black, she thought to herself. Who had her? If they had the stamp, why did they tie her up? Rachel thought about how to get out of the situation. She tried to wiggle to move in the chair and pry herself loose, but nothing worked. She slung her body back and forth until finally the chair toppled over. Her shoulder and head slammed into the concrete floor just as the door opened.

A man that looked to be in his fifties entered the room wearing all black. He had a cigar in his hand and jewelry on both hands. Two men that Rachel assumed were body guards stopped at the door and stood guard. The man in black stepped toward Rachel. "Oh, you are a fighter, aren't you?" he said with a gruff and scary voice.

Rachel glared at him, waiting to see what her captor wanted. He snapped his fingers, and two men rushed over to turn Rachel's chair upright. The men backed away and resumed their position near the door. The man in black bent down to look Rachel in the eyes. He pressed his hands on her wrists and said to her, "This can go one of two ways. We can do this the easy way, and you can tell me what I want to know, or you can refuse, and Rocco can make you tell me what I want to know."

The man snapped his fingers again and a large Italian came over to the man in black. "Remove the gag, but only if she cooperates." The man untied the bandana and pulled it from Rachel's face. She spit on the man in black's shoes. "Ah, ah, ah, ah," he warned. Rachel didn't say anything. "Where is the box?" he asked.

Rachel kept quiet and forced herself to not be terrified.

"The box. Tell me where the box is," he said in an angry tone.

"What box?" Rachel couldn't believe that came out of her mouth. She was not really interested in playing torture games with this man and his thugs.

The man slapped Rachel across the face. "Don't toy with me. Tell me where the box is."

Anger boiled inside of Rachel. She thought about the break-ins and the accident that this guy must have caused. She somehow mustered a half smirk and talked herself out of telling him where the box was. "I am a stamp collector. I don't know what you are talking about," she said.

The man snapped his fingers and his Italian muscle man put the gag back in Rachel's mouth. He tied it tight on the back and the men disappeared, slamming the door behind them. Rachel was terrified. Not only was she tied to a chair in a warehouse, but scary goons were asking her questions that she knew they would not like the answer to if she told them. And in her one chance, she had managed to make them angry. She wondered if that had been the smartest move. However, Rachel knew that in kidnappings, once the victim was taken somewhere secluded the chances of survival were about 3%. She knew she didn't have much of an opportunity to live if she didn't stall. Her only way out was to hope that the man would leave her long enough for her to either figure out a way out or for Todd to find her. She hoped Todd was looking for her. She didn't know what time it was. Had she even been gone long enough for him to notice?

The door opened again. Rachel tensed up, wondering what her next move would be. She breathed a sigh of relief as she realized it was the store owner. He walked hurriedly to her chair with some water. "I'm sorry about this. They threatened my wife. I had no choice. You have to believe me," he said pleading with Rachel.

Rachel wasn't sure if he was trying to get her to talk or if he was sincere. She decided to be overly cautious with her words. "I brought you some water and a banana, but you can't make a sound. I told them I was doing some work in the back. If they find me here, we'll both be in trouble. You have to promise to be quiet, ok?"

Rachel shook her head in agreement, still unsure of the man's intentions but determined that getting fluid and nutrition was her goal with this interaction. He untied the gag and held a bottle of water to her mouth. He helped her drink it. "Just tell them where the box is so this can be over for all of us."

Rachel started to tell the man that she had seen everyone's faces, but she didn't want to remind anyone that she was expendable. Instead, she reiterated her stance, "I don't know what box he wants."

The man was clearly frustrated with her, but he opened the banana and gave it to her a bite at a time. "Well, he knows you have it. Or at least he's convinced you do. If you don't tell him where it is, then all our gooses are cooked. Please, my wife," he begged.

Rachel believed that he was genuinely fearful for his wife. "Why didn't you call the police?"

"Call the police on Reggie Ray? Are you kidding? Do you know what he'd do to me?"

Rachel wasn't sure exactly who Reggie Ray was, but she assumed he was some sort of crime boss. "If you want to save your wife, you have to get out of here and tell someone."

"No, just tell him where the box is. He'll kill my wife if I leave. Once he has the box, he promised he'd leave us alone."

Rachel was having a hard time understanding the man's logic, but she realized everyone deals with stress in different ways. Clearly this man had lost all rational thought. There was no way a criminal that threatens an old lady and ties up another one and shows his face is going to let people walk away, but this man was not thinking clearly. "What time is it?"

"Late. After midnight, I think. You were out for a while," the man said.

At least enough time had passed that Todd would be concerned that she didn't make it back to Jimma's. Maybe he was looking for her. She hoped he was looking for her. But she didn't tell him where she was going. No, she couldn't wait on a rescue. She needed to make her own escape. "Ok, you don't have to go, just loosen the tape a little, and I'll do the rest. I'll get help."

The man stood up and immediately put the gag back on Rachel. "No! You have to cooperate! Don't you understand that he will kill us all?" The man said angrily as he tied the gag back on. "This was a mistake," he said under his breath as he left the room.

Rachel looked around at the pattern of the boxes and for another exit. She needed to know what the options were in case there was an opportunity to run. Her head pounded, and her feet were numb. Running wouldn't be the easiest thing, but she still hoped for the opportunity. She saw a door in the back corner of the room behind her. It was a long walk from the chair, but there was cover with the boxes. She hoped that whatever was in them would be enough to cover her if she needed it. She had to find a way out of the chair. She tugged on the duct tape on her arms and wiggled her feet. The tape gave in certain places, but not enough to pull free. Tears started to fall on Rachel's face. She was going to die in this warehouse if she didn't get free. She started to pray and ask for God's help to free herself, for Todd to find her, for someone to save her.

The door opened again, startling Rachel. Her tears instantly stopped flowing and anger burned within her. The man in black was back, Reggie Ray she assumed, and he had brought his body guards with him. The man walked toward Rachel and noticed her tears. He wiped her right cheek with his finger and licked the tear. Then he turned away from Rachel and started to speak, "Rachel," the man said and then turned toward her, "do you mind if I call you Rachel?" He said sarcastically and then paused slightly before turning back around. "Good. Now, Rachel, I am a reasonable man. I know you didn't steal from me, but you have found yourself in possession of something that belongs to me. I'm simply asking you to return it and all of this goes away. Are we clear?"

Rachel nodded her head in agreement. The man nodded to his muscle and the gag was removed again. "Why do you think I have a box?" Rachel asked. She really wanted to ask why he wanted the box.

"I don't think you understand. You are not in charge here. I am asking the questions, and the question is, 'where is the box?'" the man answered.

The thought scared her, but her adrenaline was pumping enough to help keep her wits about her. "I don't have a box. I have a stamp – well, I had a stamp before your goons hit me over the head."

"Yes, that was unfortunate, but my men have not been able to locate the box on their own. It's hard to find good help these days, ya know?" the man said in a polite tone. Then he snapped his head back at Rachel and angrily said, "Now tell me where the box is!"

Rachel mustered every ounce of calm she could and said, "Perhaps if you told me what box you are looking for, I could be of more help."

The man put his cigar out on the floor and handed the butt of it to one of the men. He turned back to Rachel. "Ok, you want a story. I'll tell you a story. The stamp is counterfeit. There is no such thing as the red dove. But fortunately for me, the legend almost sells itself. All I needed was a good back story and some mystery, and viola, the legend comes to life," the man said, proud of his story.

"Esther made the stamp for you," Rachel said, nodding her head.

"Of course, she did." The man snapped back. "But the greedy witch wasn't happy with what I gave her."

"So, you had J.P. kill her?"

"Nonsense. Contrary to popular belief, I do not enjoy violence. I simply suggested to my men that they persuade her to tell us where the stamp was, and well, like I said before, good help is hard to find."

"So why did J.P. take the rap for her murder?" Rachel said.

The man smiled at Rachel's desire to figure things out. "I would imagine J.P. needed to make amends for selling me a service he couldn't deliver."

"So, what does this have to do with a box?" Rachel said.

"The box? The box? The box sells the entire story. There is no stamp without the box!" the man screamed at Rachel and then began pacing around the room.

Rachel was more than confused. She wondered how a box could sell a story about a counterfeit stamp. And then suddenly, she connected the dots. The box was from Saratoga. He worked in a postal plant. He didn't steal the stamp. He just happened to have worked in the plant, and he happened to carve a box that no one had seen but whose style was notable. If this Reggie Ray could produce the stamp and have a carved box from an artist who didn't sell the box to the public, then he could convince a buyer that Saratoga stealing the stamp was plausible, and the stamp was real. Rachel still couldn't figure out how Esther got the box or why it had taken Reggie Ray so long to come looking for it. But she could figure out about how long she had to live, and that was just until they found the box. Men like Reggie Ray don't leave loose ends.

Just then, there was a knock on the door. The store owner from the collectibles shop peeked his head in. "Sir, um, we have a situation."

"Not now, Gerald!" Reggie Ray said.

A "situation" could be good news for Rachel. "But, sir the p-"

"I said not now, Gerald!" Reggie Ray shouted again and motioned to his guards. The guard on the right side of the door slammed it closed in Gerald's face. Reggie turned to Rachel. "No more stalling. Tell me where the box is!"

The door opened again, and Gerald came running through, yelling, "Sir, sir!"

One of the guards grabbed him by the collar. Reggie spun around and faced Gerald, motioning for his guards to stand down. He calmly approached Gerald and straightened his shirt out and put his arm around him. Reggie started quietly and politely as he said, "Gerald, I do not like to be interrupted. I think I have made myself very clear on that subject, haven't I?"

Gerald swallowed hard and said meekly, "Yes, sir, but —"

Reggie raised his voice and said angrily, "But what, Gerald. You just said that you know I don't like to be interrupted. So, what is it, Gerald? What could possibly be so important that you have to interrupt at this very exact moment?"

Gerald stuttered as he answered, "The-The-There is a cop out front. He is looking for her."

Rachel perked up. A cop was looking for her. It had to be Todd.

"Well, get rid of him, Gerald!" Reggie said with sarcasm, clearly frustrated at the stupidity of those around him.

"I tried, sir, but he won't leave."

"Won't leave? What did you tell him?" Reggie asked.

"He knew she was here, so I told him she came in but then she left."

"And why is he still here?" Reggie asked again, clearly more frustrated.

"I don't know. He's just wondering around the store, asking weird questions."

"Then why are you back here? Don't you think he might get just a little suspicious?"

"I told him I had some work to finish in the back," Gerald said.

Reggie put his hand up to his eye and rubbed it out of frustration. "Do I have to do everything myself?" Reggie asked as he pushed Gerald to the door. He snapped for his guards to follow.

One of the guards said, "Man, I'm not capping a cop."

Reggie stopped suddenly and glared at the man, "I just need you to get rid of him."

Reggie, Gerald, and the men started to leave the room.

Rachel thought of screaming out, but she was afraid that would make Reggie leave a man behind or put Todd in more danger. Instead she waited until the men left the room and then bent over. They had left the gag off. If she could just get to the end of the duct tape, she could set herself free. She leaned across her body and tugged on the tape with her teeth, but the tape was too strong to bite through. Rachel was instantly frustrated and fearful. She closed her eyes and prayed once again for God to protect her and Todd. She leaned back over and pulled at the side of the tape with her teeth. She couldn't tear it, but perhaps she could work enough of it off to pull herself free. She worked frantically to make headway before the men returned. The tape started to loosen as Rachel worked. After a few seconds that seemed like an eternity, she managed to get her right hand free. She quickly freed her left hand and started on her feet. She got her right foot free, but tangled the tape in her haste on her left foot. The more it twisted, the harder it became to get free.

A bang on the door startled Rachel and made her pull harder, but she still couldn't get her foot free. She started to run down the aisle of boxes with the chair in tow hoping to tear the tape with every step. The chair was heavy and moved slowly. She pulled hard and finally the tape wiggled off her ankle. She stopped to unwind it and broke her foot free from the tape. She started to run toward the door she had seen in the back of the building and then suddenly stopped when she heard gunfire. She hoped it wasn't Todd. She said a quick prayer and moved to the door. She gave it a shove, but it didn't budge. She tried again, but nothing happened. Rachel tried kicking the door, but again, it refused to budge. She turned her back and sank slowly against it, trying to figure out her next move.

If she wanted out, she would have to go out the other door, which meant going straight into harm's way. Rachel tried to consider other options. If Todd was in the building and the men hadn't come back yet, there must be a fight or standoff happening. That meant that Todd had to know she was there. She just needed somewhere to hide until he could find her.

Rachel ran up and down the aisles looking for large boxes. She located some on the second aisle to the door. She pried it open with her fingers and looked inside. It looked like old comic books, but it was only about a third full. She thought the box was large enough for her to fit into, but she wasn't sure what to do with the comic books. She pulled on the box next to it, which was considerably smaller but nearly empty. She began to transfer the books from one box to the other as fast as she could. Another shot was fired, this one closer to the door to the warehouse where she was trapped. Rachel's heart raced faster. She moved quickly. After emptying as many as she could get and still close the box, Rachel tilted the larger box toward her and started to climb inside. Suddenly the door to the warehouse opened and she could hear Reggie's voice barking orders at his men. Rachel wanted to freeze, but she needed to get out of site. She continued to climb into the box and fold the flaps in as quietly as she could. She hoped no one heard her.

"Where is the girl?" Reggie yelled. "The girl, you morons! Where did she go?"

Another man answered, "She was right here!"

"Well, she's not now. She was my ticket out of here. Without a hostage, we are sitting ducks. Find her!" Reggie yelled.

Rachel could hear the slap of the men's feet up and down the aisles. She held her breath and closed her eyes, hopeful they wouldn't find her. It seemed like several minutes before one of them spoke again. "She's not here, boss."

"She didn't just vanish! The back door is blocked. She's in this building somewhere. Find her!" Reggie yelled.

Rachel counted the seconds again, hoping for a miracle. She could feel her head becoming light. Suddenly the rush of adrenaline had worn off, and she felt sick. She hoped Todd was close to finding her. Rachel closed her eyes and prayed for God's protection. Somewhere in the middle of it, she lost consciousness, and the box tumbled out onto the floor.

Chapter 40

When Rachel came to, she was looking up at Marcus and disoriented. She blinked her eyes several times trying to get her bearings and noticed two ENT officers taking her vitals. "Welcome back, gorgeous," Marcus said.

Rachel knew it must be safe. "Todd?" she mumbled.

"Oh, I see how it's going to be. A brother rescues you from the throws of evil and you dis him for Goodie Two-Shoes Henderson. What does a man have to do around here to get a woman's respect?" Marcus joked.

Todd pushed Marcus to the side and put his hands around Rachel's face. "I'm right here, Rachel," Todd said as an ENT worker pulled him backward.

"He'll be back in a minute. I need to sew something up first," said the ENT worker as she pushed Todd out of Rachel's line of sight.

"Todd, are you ok?" Rachel managed to say loudly.

"I am now," he replied.

Rachel could hear Marcus talking in the background under his breath. "Oh, he's fine now. A minute ago, he's been shot, and the world is about to end, screaming like a little girl. Now that his girl is awake, he's all fine like some big tough guy hero."

Rachel reached for Marcus' shirt. "What? Todd was shot?" Rachel asked.

"Grazed!" Todd's voice shouted just out of her sight.

The ENT officers shined a light in her eyes and asked her some basic questions. She had a few of her own she wanted answered, but for now, being alive and safe was enough. She wasn't sure why she was so tired. Nothing seemed to hurt or be broken. She wondered what all the fuss was about, but decided to let them take her without making a scene. She closed her eyes as they loaded her into the ambulance. Todd climbed in beside her and held her hand as they sped off to the hospital.

Chapter 41

Rachel screamed for joy as she crossed the finish line. Todd laughed and said, "You know no one is here to race you, right?"

"I'm practicing for my big win!" Rachel said as she slowed the car back down and headed for the parking lot.

"Well, if you drive like that, you might have a chance to beat a pinto," Todd teased.

"Oh, come on. This car floats when it gets above 70," Rachel whined.

"I guess you are saying it's not what's under the hood or who's behind the wheel, but what's under the car that counts?"

"Something like that," Rachel said with a smile. She drove the Mustang to the top of the hill overlooking the river and turned the engine off but left the electrical part of the motor on. She turned the radio on to the local Christian station and got out of the car. Todd followed her lead.

"What a beautiful view," Rachel said looking out over the Mississippi.

Todd leaned against the car door. "I'll say," he said, staring at Rachel.

Rachel blushed, put her hands in her pocket and hunched her shoulders up to stretch her back. "You are such a flirt," she said as she leaned against the car next to Todd and listened to the radio. Weeks had passed since the stamp mystery had been solved, and Rachel had spent the time wisely, growing in her faith with Todd. For the first time in a long time, Rachel didn't need the question answered about where this was going with Todd. She liked where they were.

"Yes, I am, but only with you," Todd answered.

Suddenly, Todd got down on one knee. He held out his hand with a box in it. Rachel's heart raced uncontrollably. "Rachel Parks, will you marry me?"

Rachel put both her hands to her face. She was in total shock. They had only been dating 8 weeks. Dating. Wow, that was something she never thought she'd say about Todd. She was dating a cop. And now this? How could he possibly want to marry her?

"Todd, I –" Rachel started to say she couldn't, but the words from her conversation with Patricia came flooding back. Jump in without a life preserver and make a commitment you can't undo. Love first and always. Be the right one. Tears filled her eyes. "Are you serious?"

Todd opened the box up and revealed a stunning diamond ring. "Never more in my life than right now. Rachel, whatever days we have been given, I know God wants me to spend them with you, loving you and growing with you toward Christ. Share the journey with me. Be my perfect helpmate."

Rachel tried to say something, but nothing came out. Tears streamed down her face. Pure joy. She finally shook her head yes. Todd stood up and hugged her. Rachel wiped the tears from her eyes and took a deep breath. Todd slid the ring on her finger and smiled.

"There's just one thing I have been waiting to find out," Todd said.

"What's that?" Rachel asked, confused.

"What it's like to kiss the woman I am going to marry." Todd put his hands on her face gently and kissed her passionately, and they both knew the wait had been worth it.

Made in the USA
Middletown, DE
17 March 2018